The Serf

The Serf

by Guy Thorne

CHAPTER I

"When Christ slept"

This is the history of a man who lived in misery and torture, and was held as the very dirt of the world. In great travail of body and mind, in a state of bitter and sore distress, he lived his life. His death was stern and pitiless, for they would have slain a dog more gently than he.

And yet, while his lords and masters survive only in a few old chronicles of evil Latin, or perhaps you may see poor broken effigies of them in a very ancient church, the thoughts that Hyla thought still run down time, and have their way with us now. They seared him with heat and scourged him with whips, and hung him high against the sunset from the battlements of Outfangthef Tower, until his body fell in pieces to the fen dogs in the stable yards below. Yet the little misshapen man is worthy of a place in your hearts.

Geoffroi de la Bourne is unthought-of dust; Fulke, his son, claims fame by three lines in an old compte-book as a baron who enjoyed the right of making silver coin. In the anarchy of King Stephen's reign he coined money, using black metal—"moneta nigra"—with no small profit to himself. So he has three lines in a chronicle.

Hyla, serf and thrall to him, has had never a word of record until now.

And yet Hyla, who inspired the village community—the first Radical one might fancy him to be—was greater than Fulke or Geoffroi; and this is the Story of his life. The human heart that beat in him is even as the heart of a good man now. It will be difficult to see any lovable things in this slave, who was a murderer, and whose life was so remote from ours. But, indeed, in regarding such a man, one must remember always his environment. With a little exercise of thought you will see that he was a lovable man, a small hero and untrumpeted, but worthy of a place in a very noble hierarchy.

A man sat in a roughly-constructed punt or raft, low down among the rushes, one hot evening in June. The sun was setting in banks of blood-red light, which turned all the innumerable water-ways and pools of the fen from black to crimson. In the fierce light the tall reeds and grasses rose high into the air, like spears stained with blood.

Although there was no wind to play among the rushes and give the reeds a voice, the air was full of sound, and an enormous life palpitated and moved all round.

The marsh frogs were barking to each other with small elfin voices, and diving into the pools in play. There was a continual sucking sound, as thousands of great eels drew in the air with their heads just rising from the water. Now and again some heavy fish would leap out of the pools with a great noise, and the bitterns called to each other like copper gongs.

Very high in the air a few birds of the plover species wailed sadly to their mates, grieving that day was over.

These sounds of busy life were occasionally mingled with noises which came from the castle and village on the high grounds which bordered the fen on the south. Now and again the sound of hammers beating upon metal floated over the water, showing that they were working in the armourer's shop. A bell rang frequently, and some one was learning

The Serf

to blow calls upon a horn, for occasionally the clear, sweet notes abruptly changed into a windy lowing, like a bull in pain.

The man in the punt was busy catching eels with a pronged pole, tipped with iron. He drove the pole through the water again and again till a fish was transfixed, and added to the heap in the bottom of the boat. He was a short, thick-set fellow, with arms which were too long for his body, and huge hands and feet. No hair grew upon his face, which was heavy and without expression, though there was evidence of intelligence in the light green-grey eyes.

Round his neck a thin ring of iron was soldered, and where the two ends had been joined together another and smaller ring had been fixed. He was dressed in a coat of leather, black with age and dirt, but strong and supple. This descended almost to his knees, and was caught in round the middle by a leather strap, which was fastened with an iron pin.

His arms were bare, and on one of them, just below the fore-arm, was a red circle the size of a penny, burnt into the flesh, and bearing some marks arranged in a regular pattern.

This was Hyla, one of the serfs belonging to Geoffroi de la Bourne, Baron of Hilgay, and the holder of lands near Mortain, in France.

The absolute anarchy of the country in 1136,—the dark age in which this story of Hyla begins—secured to each petty baron an overwhelming power, and Geoffroi de la Bourne was king, in all but name, of the fens, hills, and corn-lands, from Thorney to Thetford, and the undoubted lord of the Southfolk.

For many miles the fens spread under the sky from Ely to King's Lynn, then but a few fisher huts. Hilgay itself rose up on an eminence towards the south of the Great Fen. At the bottom of the hill ran the wide river Ouse, and beyond it stretched the treacherous wastes.

The Castle of Hilgay stood on the hill itself, and was surrounded by a small village, built in the latter years of Henry's reign. It was one of the most modern buildings in East Anglia. Here, surrounded by his men-at-arms, villeins, and serfs, Geoffroi de la Bourne lived secure, and kept the country-side in stern obedience. The Saxon Chronicle, which at the time was being written in the Monastery of Peterborough, says of him: "He took all those he thought had any goods, both by night and day, men and women alike, and put them in prison to get their gold and silver, and tortured them with tortures unspeakable."

Of he and his kind it says: "Never yet was there such misery in the land; never did heathen men worse than they. Christ slept, and all His saints."

Hyla had been spearing his eels in various backwaters and fen-pools which wound in and out from the great river. When his catch was sufficient, he laid down the trident, and, taking up the punt pole, set seriously about the business of return. The red lights of the sky turned opal and grew dim as he sent his punt gliding swiftly in and out among the rushes.

After several minutes of twisting and turning, the ditch widened into a large, still pool, over which the flies were dancing, and beyond it was the black expanse of the river itself. As the boat swung out into the main stream, the castle came plain to the view. A well-beaten road fringed with grass, among which bright golden kingcups were shining, led up to the walls. Clustered round the walls was a little village of sheds, huts, and houses, where the labourers and serfs who were employed on the farm-lands lived.

The castle itself was a massive and imposing place, of great strength and large area. At one corner of the keep stood a great tower, the highest for many miles round, which was covered with a pointed roof of tiles, like that of a French chateau. This was known as the

The Serf

Outfangthef Tower, and Geoffroi and his daughter, Lady Alice, had their private chambers in it.

There was something very stately in the view from the river, all irradiated as it was by the ruddy evening light.

Hyla's punt glided over the still waters till it reached a well-built landing-stage of stone steps descending into the river. Several punts and boats were tied up to mooring stakes. Hard by, the sewage from the castle was carried down by a little brook, and the air all about the landing-place was stagnant and foul.

He moored the punt, and, stringing his eels upon an iron hook, carried them up the hill in the waning light. The very last lights of the day were now expiring, and the scene was full of peace and rest, as night threw her cloak over the world. A rabbit ran across Hyla's path from side to side of the road, a dusky flash; and, high up in the air, a bird suddenly began to trill the night a welcome.

The man walked slowly, lurching along with his head bent down, and seeing nothing of the evening time. About half-way up the hill he heard someone whistling a comic song, with which a wandering minstrel had convulsed the inmates of the castle a night or or two before.

Sitting by the roadside in the dusk, he could distinguish the figure of Pierce, one of the men-at-arms. He was oiling the trigger and barrel of a cross-bow, and polishing the steel parts with a soft skin. The man-at-arms lived in the village with his wife, and was practically in the position of a villein, holding some fields from Lord Geoffroi in return for military service. He was from Boulogne, and had been in the garrison of one of Robert de Bellême's castles in Normandy.

The lessons learnt at Tenchebrai had sunk deep into the mind of this fellow; and when any dirty work was afoot or any foul deed to be done, to Pierce was given the doing of it. As Hyla approached, he stopped his whistling, and broke out into the words of the song, which, filthy and obscene as it was, had enormous popularity all over the country-side.

Then he noticed the serf's approach. "Who are you?" he called out in a *patois* of Norman-French and English, with the curious see-saw of French accentuation in his voice.

"Hyla!" came the answer, and there was strength and music in it.

Something seemed to tickle the soldier to immediate merriment when he heard the identity of the man with the eels.

Hyla knew him well. When he was free from his duties in the castle, Hyla and his wife worked in this man's fields for a loaf of wastel bread or a chance rabbit, and he was in a sense their immediate employer and patron.

It was at the order of Pierce that Hyla had been fishing that evening. The soldier chuckled on, regarding the serf with obvious amusement, though for what reason *he* could not imagine.

"Show your catch," he said at last.

He was shown the hook of great eels, some of which still writhed slowly in torture.

"Take them to my wife," said the soldier, "and take what you want of them for yourself and your people."

"Very gladly," said Hyla, "for there are many mouths to fill."

"Oh! that can be altered," said the soldier, with a grin; "your family can be used in other ways, and live in other housen than under your roof-tree."

"Duke Christ forbid!" said Hyla, giving the Saviour the highest name he knew; "had I not my children and my wife, I should be poor indeed."

The Serf

"God's teeth!" cried the soldier, with a nasty snarl and complete change of tone, "*your* wife, *your* girls! Man, man! we have been too good to the serfs of late. See to this now, when I was in the train of my Lord de Bellême, both in France and here, we killed serfs like rabbits.

"Well I remember, in the Welsh March, how we hanged men like you up by the feet, and smoked them with foul smoke. Some were hanged up by their thumbs, others by the head, and burning things were hung on to their feet. We put knotted strings about their heads, and writhed them till they went into the brain. We put men into prisons where adders, snakes, and toads were crawling, and so we tormented them. And the whiles we took their wives and daughters for our own pleasure. Hear you that, Hyla, my friend? Get you off to my wife with the eels, you old dog."

He blazed his bold eyes at the serf, and his swarthy face and coal-black hair seemed bristling with anger and disdain. His face was deeply pitted with marks which one of the numerous varieties of the plague had left upon it, and as his white, strong teeth flashed in anger through the gloom, he looked, so Hyla thought, like the grinning devil-face of stone carved over the servants' wicket at Icombe Abbey.

He slunk away from the man-at-arms without a word, and toiled on up the hill. He fancied he could hear Pierce laughing down below him, and he spat upon the ground in impotent rage.

He soon came to a few pasture fields on the outskirts of the village, some parts of them all silver-white with "lady-smocks." Hardy little cows, goats, and sheep roamed in the meadows, which were enclosed with rough stone walls. A herd of pigs were wallowing in the mud which lined the banks of the sewage stream, for, with their usual ignorance, the castle architects allowed this to run right through the pastures on the hill slope.

The cows were lowing uneasily to each other, for they were tormented by hosts of knats and marsh-begotten flies which rose up from the fen below.

Past the fields the road widened out into a square of yellow, dust-powdered grass—the village green—and round this were set some of the principal houses.

There was no room for comfortable dwelling-places inside the castle itself for the crowd of inferior officers and men-at-arms. Accordingly they made their home in the village at its walls, and could retreat into safety in times of war.

Eustace, the head armourer, had a house here, the best in the village, roofed with shingle and built of solid timber. The men-at-arms, Pierce among them, who were married, or lived with women taken in battle, had their dwellings there; and one thatched Saxon house belonged to Lewin, the worker in metal, and chief of Baron Geoffroi's mint.

Hyla was a labourer in the mint, and under the orders of Lewin the Jew.

In 1133 it was established as a general truth and legal adage, by the Justiciar of England himself, that no subject might coin silver money. The adulteration practised in the baronial mints had reduced coins, which pretended to be of silver, into an alloy which was principally composed of a bastard copper. A few exceptions were made to the law, but all private mints were supposed to be under the direct superintendence of crown officials. In the anarchy of Stephen's reign this rule became inoperative, and many barons and bishops coined money for themselves.

Few did this so completely and well as Geoffroi de la Bourne.

When Bishop Roger of Salisbury made his son Chancellor of the Exchequer, in King Henry's reign, the chancellor had in his train a clever Jew boy, baptised by force, very skilful in the manual arts.

It was the youth Lewin who invented the cloth, chequered like a chess-board, which covered the table of the "Exchequer," and on which money was counted out; and he also claimed that the "tallies" which were given in receipt for taxes to the county sheriffs were a product of his fertile brain.

This man, was always looked upon with suspicion by the many churchmen with whom he came in contact. Finance was almost entirely in the hands of the great clergymen, and the servant Lewin was distrusted for his cleverness and anti-Christian blood. At dinner many a worthy bishop would urge the chancellor to dismiss him.

The Jew was too shrewd not to feel their hostility and know their dislike; and when he came across Geoffroi de la Bourne in the Tower Royal, where Cheapside now stands, he was easily persuaded to enter his service.

At Hilgay Castle he was at the head of a fine organisation of metal-workers, and under the direct protection of a powerful chief. So lawless was the time that he could gratify the coarse passions of his Eastern blood to the full, and he counted few men, and certainly no other Jew in East England, more fortunately circumstanced than he was.

A few villeins of the farmer class, who were also skilled men at arms, had rough houses in the village, and tilled the corn-fields and looked after the cattle. Beyond their dwellings, on the verge of the woods of oak and beech which purpled the southern distance, were the huts of the serfs.

Hyla passed slowly through the village. On the green, by a well which stood in the centre, a group of light-haired Saxon women were chattering over their household affairs. At the doors of some of the houses of the Norman men-at-arms sat French women on stools, rinsing pot herbs and scouring iron cooking bowls. Their black hair, prominent noses, and alert eyes contrasted favourably with the somewhat stupid faces of the Saxons, and there could be seen in them more than one sign of a conquering race.

They were also more neatly dressed, and a coarse flax linen bound their temples in its whiteness, or lay about their throats.

Stepping over a gutter full of evil-smelling refuse, Hyla came to the house of Pierce, and beat upon the wooden door, which hung upon hinges of leather made from bullock's hide.

It swung open, and Adelais, the soldier's wife, named after the Duke of Brabant's daughter, stood upon the threshold obedient to the summons.

She took the eels from him without a word, and began to unhook them.

"Pierce said that I might have some fish to take home," Hyla told her humbly.

"You may take your belly full," she answered; "it's little enough I like the river worms, for that is all they are. My man likes them as little as I."

"It was he that sent me a-fishing," said Hyla in surprise.

"Then he had a due reason," said the woman; "but get you home, the evening is spent, and the night comes."

Just then, from the castle above their heads, which towered up into the still warm air, came the mellow sound of a horn, and following upon it the deep tolling of a bell ringing the curfew.

Although the evening bell did not ring at that time with any legal significance as it did in towns, its sound was generally a signal for sleep; and as the brazen notes floated above them, the groups at the doors and on the green broke up and dispersed.

"Sleep well, Hyla!" Adelais said kindly, and, retiring into the house, she shut her door.

Hyla went on till he came opposite the great gate of the castle, and could hear the guards being changed on the other side of the drawbridge.

He was now on the very brow of the hill, and, stopping for a moment, looked right down over the road he had traversed. The moon was just rising, and the road was all white in its light. Far beyond, the vast fens were a sea of white mist, and the blue will-o'-the-wisp was beginning to bob and pirouette among it. The air of the village was full of the sweet pungent smell of the blue wood smoke.

The night was full of peace and sweetness, and, as the last throbbing note of the curfew bell died away, it would have been difficult to find a gentler, mellower place.

Thin lines of lights, like jewels in velvet, began to twinkle out in the black walls of the castle as he turned towards the place of the serfs. He went down a lane fringed with beeches, and emerged upon the open glade. A fire was burning in the centre, and dark forms were flitting round it cooking the evening meals. Dogs were barking, and there was a continual hum and clatter of life.

Picture for yourself an oblong space surrounded by heavy trees, the outer boles being striped clear of bark, and many of them remaining but dead stumps.

Round the arena stood forty or fifty huts of wood, wattled with oziers and thatched with fern and dried rushes.

Many of the huts were built round a tree trunk, and the pole in the middle served to hang skins and implements upon by means of wooden pegs driven into it.

A hole in the roof let out smoke, and in the walls let in the light. The floors of these huts were of hard-beaten earth, as durable as stone; but they were littered with old bones, dust, and dried rushes for several inches deep, and swarming with animal life.

They were the merest shelters, and served only for sleep. Most of the household business was conducted in the open before the huts, and in fine weather the fires were nearly all outside. In winter time the serf women and girls generally suffered from an irritating soreness of the eyes, which was produced by living in the acrid smoke which filled the shelters and escaped but slowly through the roofs.

The household utensils were few and simple. A large wooden bucket, which was carried on a pole between two women, served to fetch water from the well upon the village green, for the serfs had no watering-place in their own enclosure. An earthenware pot or so—very liable to break and crack, as it was baked from the black and porous fen clay—and an iron cooking pot, often the common property of two or more families, comprised the household goods.

They slept in the back part of the huts, men, women, and children together, on dried fern, or with, perhaps, an old and filthy sheep's skin for cover. The sleeping-room was called the "bower."

This enclosure where the theows lived was known as the "fold," as it was fenced in from the forest, on which it abutted, by felled trees. This was done for protection against wild beasts. Herds of wild and savage white cattle, such as may now only be seen at Chillingham, roamed through the wood. Savage boars lived on the forest acorns, and would attack an unarmed man at sight. Wolves abounded in the depths of the forest. It often happened that some little serf child wandered away, and was never seen again, and it was useless for a thrall to attempt escape into its mysterious depths.

For the most part only married serfs lived in the fold or "stoke," as it was sometimes called. Many of the younger men were employed as grooms and water-carriers in the castle, or slept and lived in sheds and cattle houses belonging to the men-at-arms and farmers in the village.

It was thus that the serfs lived, and Hyla skirted the fold till he came to his own house. He was very tired and hungry, and eager for a meal before sleeping.

All the morning he had laboured, sweating by the glowing fires of the mint, pouring molten metal into the moulds. At mid-day the steward had given him a vessel of spoilt black barley for his wife to bake bread, and he had taken it home to her and his two daughters against his return.

In the afternoon Hyla and his two daughters, Frija and Elgifu, girls of twenty and nineteen, had been at work dunging the fields of Pierce the man-at-arms, and the evening had been spent, as we have seen, in spearing eels.

Hyla was very weary and hungry. When he came up to his hut he saw angrily that the fire in front of it was nothing but dead embers, and, indeed, was long since cold. His two little sons, who were generally tumbling about naked by the hut, were not there, nor could he see Gruach his wife.

He flung down the eels in a temper, and called aloud, in his strong voice, "Frija! Elgifu! Gruach!"

His cries brought no response, and he turned towards the fire in the centre of the stoke which was now but a red glow, and round which various people were sitting eating their evening meal.

He burst into the circle. "Where is Gruach?" he said to a young man who was dipping his hand into an earthen pot held between his knees.

This was Harl, an armourer's rivetter, who generally lived within the castle walls.

"Gruach is at the hut of Cerdic," he said, with some embarrassment, and, so it seemed to Hyla, with pity in his voice.

The men and women sitting by the fire turned their faces towards him without exception, and their faces bore the same expression as Harl's.

Hyla stared stupidly from one to the other. His eyes fell upon Cerdic himself, a kennel serf, and something of a veterinary surgeon. It was he who cut off two toes from each dog used for droving, so that they should not hunt the deer.

Fastened to his girdle was the ring through which the feet of the "lawed" dogs were passed, and he carried his operating knife in a sheath at his side.

"My woman is in your hut, Cerdic," said Hyla, "and why is she with?"

"She is with," said Cerdic, "because she is in sore trouble, and walks in fear of worse. Go you to her, Hyla, and hear her words, and then come you here again to me."

A deep sigh burst from all of them as Cerdic spoke, and one woman fell crying.

Hyla turned, and strode hastily to Cerdic's hut. He heard a low moaning coming from it, which rose and fell unceasingly, and was broken in upon by a woman's voice cooing kind words of comfort.

He pushed into the hut. It was quite dark and full of fœtid smoke and a most evil odour.

"Gruach," he said, "Gruach! why are you not home? What hurts you?"

The moaning stopped, and there was a sound of some one rising.

Then a voice, which Hyla recognised as belonging to Cerdic's wife, said, "Here is your man, Gruach! Rise and tell him what bitter things have been afoot."

Gruach rose, a tall woman of middle age, and came out of the hut into the twilight.

"Hyla!" she said, "Saints help you and me, for they have taken Elgifu and Frija to the castle."

The man quivered all over as if he would have fallen on the ground. Then he gripped his wife's arm. "Tell me," he said hoarsely, "To the castle? to the castle? Frija and Elgifu?"

"Aye, your maids and mine, and maids no longer. I had gone to Adelais to seek food for this night, and found you sent a-fishing. Frija and Elgifu were carrying the dung to the fields. Pierce was in the field speaking to our girls. Then came Huber and John from the castle with their pikes, and they took away our daughters, saying Lord Geoffroi and Lord Fulke had sent for them. Huber struck me in the face at my crying. 'Take care!' cwaeth he, 'old women are easily flogged; there is little value in you.' And I saw them holding my girls, and they took them in the great gate of the castle laughing, and I did not see them again."

Hyla said nothing for a minute, but remained still and motionless. The blow struck him too hard for speech.

"Get you home," he said at length, "if perchance you may fall asleep. I am going to talk with Cerdic. Take her home, wife, and God rest you for your comfort!"

He walked quickly across the open space back to the fire. The circle was broken up, and only Cerdic and Harl sat there waiting Hyla's return.

Stuck into the ground was a cow's horn full of ale, and as Hyla came into the circle of dim red light, Harl handed it to him.

He drank deep, and drank again till the comfort of the liquor filled his craving stomach, and his brain grew clearer.

"Sit here, friend," said Cerdic. "This is a foul thing that has been done."

CHAPTER II

"Coelum coeli Domino terram autem dedit filiis hominum."

In the fifth volume of an instructive work by Le Grand d'Aussy, who was, in his way, a kind of inferior Dean Swift, there is an interesting story, one of a collection of "Fabliaux."

There was once a genial ruffian who lived by highway robbery, but who, on setting about his occupation, was careful to address a prayer to the Virgin. He was taken at the end, and sentenced with doom of hanging. While the executioner was fitting him with the cord, he made his usual little prayer. It proved effectual. The Virgin supported his feet "with her white hands," and thus kept him alive two days to the no small surprise of the executioner, who attempted to complete his work with a hatchet. But this was turned aside by the same invisible hand, and the executioner bowed to the miracle, and unstrung the robber. With that—very naturally—the rogue entered a monastery.

In another tale the Virgin takes the shape of a nun, who had eloped from the convent where she was professed, and performs her duties for ten years. At last, tired of a libertine life, the nun returned unsuspected. This signal service was performed in consideration of the nun's having never omitted to say an *Ave* as she passed the Virgin's image.

These stories are perfectly fair examples of monastic teachings in the Twelfth Century. Roughly speaking, any one might do anything if he or she said an occasional Ave. *Indeed, Dom Mathew Paris, the most pious and trustworthy monkish historian, and in his way a scourge to the laxity of his own order, has more than one story of this kind in which he evidently believes.*

It may be therefore said, without exciting any undue surprise, that Geoffroi de la Bourne had a resident chaplain in the castle, one Dom Anselm, and that religious ceremonies were more or less regularly observed.

In the outer courtyard of the castle a doorway led into the chapel. This was a long room, with a roof of vaulted stone lit by windows on the courtyard side, full of some very presentable stained glass. The glass, which had far more lead in it than ours, was

in fact a kind of mosaic, and the continual lattice work of metal much obscured the pattern.

What could be seen of it, however, represented Saint Peter armed, and riding out to go hawking, with a falcon on his wrist.

Strips of cloth bandaged cross-wise from the ankle to the knee, and fastened over red stockings, were part of the saint's costume, and he wore black-pointed shoes split along the instep almost to the toes, fastened with two thongs.

In fact, the artists of that day were under the influence of a realistic movement, in much the same way as the exhibitors in the modern French salon, and what superficial students of Twelfth-Century manners put down as unimaginative ignorance was really the outcome of a widely understood artistic pose.

On a shrine by the chapel door stood an image of the Blessed Virgin, a trifle gaudy. The head was bound round with a linen veil, and a loose gown of the same material was laced over a tight-fitting bodice. Round the arms were wound gold snake bracelets, imitations, made by Lewin in the forge, of some old Danish ornaments in the possession of the Lady Alice de la Bourne. The foldings of the robe were looped up here and there with jewelled butterflies, differing not at all from a Palais Royal toy of to-day.

In front of the shrine hung two lamps, or "light vats" as they were called, of distinctly Roman type—luxuries which were rare then, and of which Dom Anselm was exceedingly proud. They dated from the time of King Alfred, that inventive monarch, who had adapted the idea of lamps from old Roman relics found in excavations.

Except that the altar furniture was in exceedingly good taste, it differed hardly at all from anything that may be seen in twenty London churches to-day.

There were no pews or seats in the chapel, save some heavy oak chairs by the altar side, where a wooden perch, clamped to the table itself and white with guano, indicated that Geoffroi de la Bourne would sit with his hawks.

The sun rose in full June majesty the next morning, and soon shone upon the picturesque activity of a mediæval fortress in prosperous being.

The serfs and workmen, who slept in lightly constructed huts of thin elm planks under a raised wooden gallery which went round the courtyard, rose from the straw in which they lay with the dogs, and, shaking themselves, set about work.

The windlass of the well creaked and groaned as the water for the horses was drawn. The carpenters began their labour of cutting boards for some new mead-benches which were wanted in the hall, and men began to stoke afresh the furnaces of the armoury and mint.

Paved ways ran from door to door of the various buildings, but all the rest of the bailey was carpeted with grass, which had been sown there to feed the cattle who would be herded within the walls in dangerous times.

About half-past eight Dom Anselm let himself out of a little gate in the corner of Outfangthef Tower, and came grumbling down the steps. He crossed the courtyard, taking no notice of the salutations of the labourers, but looking as if he were half asleep, as indeed he was. His long beard was matted and thick with wine-stains from the night before, and his thin face was an unhealthy yellow colour.

He unlocked the chapel door, and mechanically pushed a dirty thumb into a holy water stoup. Then he bowed low to the monstrance on the altar, and lower still to the figure of the Virgin. After the hot sunshine of the outside world, the chapel was chill and damp, and the air struck unpleasantly upon him.

He went up to the altar to find his missal. Sleeping always in a filthy little cell with no ventilation, and generally seeking his bed in a state of intoxication, had afflicted the priest with a chronic catarrh of the nose and throat—as common a complaint among the priesthood then as it is now in the country districts of Italy and southern France. Quite regardless of his environment, he expectorated horribly even as he bowed to the presence of Christ upon the altar.

It is necessary for an understanding of those times to make a point of things, which, in a tale of contemporary events, would be unseemly and inartistic. Dom Anselm saw nothing amiss with his manners, and the fact helps to explain Dom Anselm and his brethren to the reader.

With a small key the priest opened a strong box banded with bronze, and drew from it the vessels.

Among the contents of the box were some delicate napkins which Lady Alice had worked—some of those beautiful pieces of embroidery which were known all over Europe as "English work."

When the silver vessels were placed upon the altar, and everything was ready for the service, the thirst of the morning got firm hold upon Dom Anselm's throat.

He left the chapel, and summoned a theow who was passing the door with a great bundle of cabbages in his arm.

"Set those down," he said, "and ring the bell for Mass;" and while the man obeyed, and the bell beat out its summons to prayer—very musical in the morning air—he strode across the courtyard to the mint.

By this time, in the long, low buildings, the fires were banked up, the tools lay ready upon the benches, and the men were greasing the moulds with bacon fat.

The priest went through the room with two raised fingers, turning quickly and mechanically towards the toil-worn figures who knelt or bowed low for his blessing. He walked towards an inner room, the door of which was hung with a curtain of moth-eaten cat-skin—the cheapest drapery of the time. Pushing this curtain aside, he entered with a cheery "Good-day!" to find, as he expected, Lewin, the mint-master.

The Jew was a slim man of middle size, clean-shaven, and with dark-red hair. His face was handsome and commanding, and yet animal. The wolf and pig struggled for mastery in it. He was engaged in opening the brass-bound door of a recess or cupboard in the wall, where the dies for stamping coin were kept in strict ward.

The mint-master straightway called to one of the men in the outer room, who thereon brought in a great horn of ale in the manner of use. Every morning the priest would call upon the Jew, so that they might take their drink together. Each day the two friends conveniently forgot—or at any rate disregarded—the rule which bids men fast before the Mass. Lewin attended Church with great devotion, and, like many modern Israelites, was most anxious that the fact of his ancient and honourable descent should be forgotten.

Though he himself was a professing Christian, and secure in his position, yet his brethren, who nearly always remained staunch to their ancient faith, were in very sad case in the Twelfth Century. Vaissette, in his history of Languedoc, dwells upon a pleasing custom which obtained at Toulouse, to give a blow on the face to a Jew every Easter. In some districts of England, from Palm Sunday to Easter was regarded as a licensed time for the baiting of Jews, and the populace was regularly instigated by the priests to attack Jewish houses with stones. Yet, at the same time, it was possible for a Jew to obtain a respectable position if he avoided the practice of usury, and Lewin the minter was an example of the fact.

"This is the best beer of the day," said the priest, "eke the beer at noon meat. My belly is so hot in the morning, and all the pipes of my body burn."

Lewin poured out some ale from the horn into a Saxon drinking-glass with a rounded bottom like a modern soda-water bottle—the invariable pattern—and handed the horn back to Dom Anselm. They drank simultaneously with certain words of pledge, and clinked the vessels together.

"It's time for service," said the clergyman, when the horn was empty. "Lady Alice will be upon arriving and in a devilish temper, keep I her waiting."

"Lord Geoffroi," said Lewin, "will he be at Mass?"

The priest grinned with an evil smile. "What do you think, minter?" he chuckled. "Geoffroi never comes to Mass when he sins a mortal sin o'er night; no, nor young Fulke either."

Lewin looked enquiringly at him.

"Two of the men-at-arms brought the daughters of one Hyla into the castle last night before curfew."

"He works for me here," said the minter.

"I am sorry for him," said the priest, "and I do not like this force, for the girls were screaming as they took them to Outfangthef. Lord Christ forbid that I should ever take from a maiden what she would not give. It will mean candles of real wax for me from Geoffroi, this will."

"The master is a stern man," said Lewin as they entered the chapel door.

Lady Alice was already in the chapel, kneeling on the altar steps, and behind her were two or three maids also kneeling.

On the eyelids of one of these girls the tears still stood glistening, and a red mark upon her cheek showed that Lady Alice had not risen in the best of tempers. The chatelaine frowned at Anselm when she heard his footsteps, and, turning, saw him robing by the door.

Many of the workmen and men-at-arms crowded into the chapel, all degrees mingling together. Some of the villein farmers had come in from the village, sturdy, open-featured men, prosperously dressed in woollen tunics reaching to the knees, fastened with a brooch of bone. The serfs knelt at the back, and as the deep pattering Latin rolled down the church every head was bent low in reverence.

Although among nearly all of them there was such a contrast between conduct and belief, yet, at the daily mystery and miracle of the Mass, every evil brain was filled with reverence and awe. When the Host was raised—the very body of Christ—to them all, you may judge how it moved every human heart.

The system which held them all was a very easy and pleasant system. Unconditional submission to the Church, and belief in her mysteries, ensured the redemption of sins and the joys of heaven hereafter. To the popular mind, my Lords the Saints and the Blessed Virgin were great, good-humoured people, always approachable by an *Ave* and a little private understanding with the priest. It was, indeed, the pleasantest and easiest of all religious systems.

This, then, was the ordinary attitude of men and women towards the unseen, and it helps to explain the wickedness of the time. Yet it must not be thought that in this dark tapestry there were no lighter threads. The saints of God were still to be found on earth. Bright lines of gold and white and silver ran through the warp and woof, and we shall meet with more than one fine and Christian character in this story of Hyla.

The stately monotone went on. Huber and John, the two men-at-arms who had hurried the poor serf girls into the castle the night before, knelt in reverence, and beat their breasts.

"The Lord is debonair," Huber muttered to himself. Alice de la Bourne forgot her ill temper and petty dislike of pretty Gundruda, her maid, and fervently made the sign of the cross. Lewin alone, of all that kneeling throng, was uninfluenced by the ceremony and full of earthly thoughts.

After Mass was over, Anselm remained kneeling, repeating prayers, while the congregation filed out into the sunlight. A little significant incident happened on the very threshold. A poor serf had become possessed of a rosary made from the shells of a pretty little pink and green snail which was found—not too frequently—in the marshes below. This possession of his he valued, and, as he said his prayers day by day, it became invested with a mystical importance. He looked on it as a very holy thing.

Coming out of church, among the last of the crowd, he let it fall upon the step of the door. He was stooping to pick it up, when he came in the way of Huber, the soldier, who sent him flying into the courtyard with a hearty kick.

The soldier stepped upon the rosary, breaking most of the shells, and then picked it up in some curiosity. He had it in his hand, and was showing it to his companions, when the serf, who had risen from the ground, leapt upon him in anger.

There was an instant scuffle, and a loud explosion of oaths. In a second or two three or four men held the unhappy serf by the arms, and had fastened him up to the post of the well in the centre of the yard. They tied him up with two or three turns of the well rope, which they unhooked from the bucket.

Huber took his leather belt and flogged him lustily, after his tunic of cat-skin had been pulled down to the waist. The wretch screamed for mercy, and attracted all the workmen round, who stood watching—the serfs in timid silence, and the men-at-arms with mirth and laughter. It may sound incredible, but Lady Alice herself, standing on the top step of the stairway leading to the tower door, watched with every sign of amusement. It was, in fact, no uncommon thing in those cruel times for great Norman and Saxon ladies to order their slaves to be horribly tortured on the slightest provocation. Cruelty seemed an integral part of their characters. There is, for example, a well-attested story of Ethelred's mother, who struck him so heavily with a bunch of candles which lay to her hand, that he fell senseless for near an hour.

Dom Anselm came out of chapel after a while, and sought the cause of the uproar.

"There, my men," he said, "let the theow go. Whatever he has done, he has paid toll now. And look to it, Henry, that you say an *Ave* to our Blessed Lady that you harbour no wrath towards your just lords."

With that they let him go, and, bleeding and sobbing, the poor fellow slunk away into the stables. Sitting in the straw, he cried as if his heart would break, until he felt hot breath on his cheek, and looking up saw large mild eyes, like still woodland pools, regarding him with love. Above him towered the vast form of "Duke Robert," Geoffroi's great war charger, as large and ponderous as a small elephant, his one dear friend. So he forgot his troubles a little while.

It was now about nine o'clock, and breakfast was served. The Baron and his son, and also the Lady Alice, never appeared in the great hall until the "noon meat" at three. They ate the first meal of the day in the "bowers" or sleeping chambers.

While the Lady Alice and her women superintended the more important household business, or sat in the orchard outside the south wall of the castle with their needlework, the Baron was throned in the gateway of the castle conducting the business of his estate, and presiding over a kind of local court.

The Justices in Eyre were hardly yet sufficiently established on circuit, and, moreover, the country was in so disturbed a state that the administration of law was merely in most cases, certainly at Hilgay, a question of local tyranny.

The whole business of the day was well afoot with all its multifarious activity when Hyla rested from his work, and sitting under the shadow of a stone wall, ate a hunk of bread which he had brought with him. He had sat late with Cerdic the night before, and, as he had half expected, had been bidden in the morning to work in Pierce's fields, and not to go to the castle. All the morning, since early dawn, he had been manuring fields with marl, in the old British fashion. The work was very hard, as the fields were only in the first stage of being reclaimed from wild common land, and required infinite preparation.

The supply of dung had given out, and the marl was hard to carry and bad to breathe.

The awful blow dealt to his whole life had dazed his brain for hours, but the long talk with Cerdic and Harl had condensed his pain within him, and turned it to strong purpose.

He thought over his life as he remembered it, his dull life of slavery, and saw with bitter clearness how the clouds were gathering round him and his kind. The present and the future alike were black as night, and the years pressed more and more heavily as they dragged onwards.

During the last years the serfs at Hilgay had been more ill-used and down-trodden than ever before. The Saxon gentlemen, who had held the forefathers of Hyla in thrall, were stern and hard, but life had been possible with them. Life was more light-hearted. Githa would sometimes dance upon the green when the day's work was done, and spend a few long-hoarded triens in an ivory comb or a string of coloured beads.

The Gesith or Thanes, the lesser nobility, had not been unkind to their slaves, and there was sometimes a draught of "pigment" for them—a sweet liquor, made of honey, wine, and spice—at times of festival.

Now everything was changed, and among the serfs a passionate spirit of hatred and revolt was springing up. The less intelligent of them sank into the condition of mere beasts of burden, without soul or brain. On the other hand, adversity had sharpened the powers of others, and in many of them was being born the first glimmerings of a consciousness that even they had rights.

Hyla himself was one of the most advanced among his brethren. He felt his manhood and "individuality" more than most of them. "I am I" his brain sometimes whispered to him. The cruel oppressions to which he was subject roused him more poignantly day by day.

Some nine months before a peculiarly atrocious deed had consolidated the nebulous and unexpressed sense of revolt among the serfs of Hilgay into a regular and definite subject of conversation.

The Forest Laws, which Knut had fenced round with a number of ferocious edicts, placing the deer and swine far above the serfs themselves, were made even more vigorous and harsh by the Normans. A theow named Gurth, who had been seen by a forester picking wood for fires, was suspected of killing a young boar, which had been found not long after with its belly ripped open by a sharp stake. Parts of the animal had been cut away, obviously by a knife, and were missing. Although the serf was absolutely innocent of the beast's slaughter, which was purely accidental—he had come upon it dead in the forest, and taken a forequarter to his home—Geoffroi de la Bourne burnt him in the centre of the village, and flogged mercilessly all the serfs, women included, who were thought to have partaken of the dish.

Since that time the men-at-arms and inferior followers of the castle had taken license to ill-use the serfs in every possible way. The virtue of no comely girl or married woman was safe, floggings were of daily occurrence, and, as there were plenty of theows to work, nothing was said if one or two were occasionally killed or maimed for life in a drunken brawl.

The serfs in the castle itself had no thoughts but of submission; but those who lived in the stoke, mingling freely with each other, and with the poor freedom of their own huts and wives, began to meet night by night round the central fire to discuss their wrongs.

The Normans never went into the stoke, or at least very rarely. The theows could not escape, and so that they did the tasks set them, their proceedings at night mattered not at all.

Hyla sat munching his manchet, and drinking from a horn of sour Welsh ale, a thin brew staple to the common people. The thought of Frija and Elgifu was almost more than he could bear.

It is interesting to note that Hyla's passionate anger was directed entirely against his masters. He had never known a spiritual revolt. It never entered his head to imagine that the God to whom he prayed had much to do with the state of the world. He never supplicated for bodily relief in his prayers, but only for pardon for his sins and for hope of heaven. The principalities and powers of the other world were too awful and mysterious, he thought, to have any actual bearing upon life.

The dominant idea of his brain was a lust for revenge, and yet it was by no means a *personal* revenge. He was full of pity for his friends, for all the serfs, and his own miseries were only as a drop in the cup of his wrath.

Night by night the serfs had begun to sit in the stoke holding conclave. It was an ominous gathering for those in high places! Hyla was generally the speaker of these poor parliaments. "HE went after the herons this noon, with Lady Alice and the squires," one man would say, provoking discussion.

"Yes," Hyla might answer, "and his falcon had t' head in a broidered hood eke a peal of silver bells. Never a bonnet of fine cloth for you, Harl; you are no bird."

"He rode over Oswald's field of ripening corn, and had noon meat with all his train at the farm."

"That is the law for a lord. Or—"

"I was at the hall door, supper time, among the lecheurs. Lord Fulke he did call me, and bade me fetch the board for chess and the images, having in his mind to game with Brian de Burgh. He broke the board on my head when I knelt with it, for he said I had the ugliest face he ever saw."

"Lord Christ made your face," would come from Cerdic or Hyla, and the ill-favoured one would finger his scars with more resentment than ever.

This man Cerdic was a born agitator. Without the dogged sincerity of Hyla, he had a readier tongue and a more commanding presence. His own injuries were the mainspring of his actions, for he had once been a full ceorl, with bocland of his own. From yeoman to serf was a terrible drop in the social scale. As a ceorl, Cerdic had a freeman's right of bearing arms, and could have reasonably hoped to climb up, by years of industry and fortunate speculation, into the ranks of the Gesith or Thanes. Speculation, indeed, proved his ruin, and debt was the last occasion of his downfall. He was nearly sixty now, and a slave who could own no property, take no oath, complete no document.

As Hyla sat in the sun he saw Cerdic coming towards him, followed by a little frisking crowd of puppies. The lawer of dogs sat him down beside his friend, and, taking out his knife, began to whet it upon a hone.

"It's a sure thing, then?" he said to Hyla. "You are certain in purpose, Hyla? You will do it indeed? Remember, eftsoons you said that it was in you to strike a blow for us all; but it's a fool's part to fumble with Satan his tail. Are you firm?"

He took one of the little dogs between his knees, a pretty, frisking little creature, thinking nothing of its imminent pain, and, holding one of its fore-paws in his hand, picked up the knife. The puppy whined piteously as the swift scalpel divided the living gristle of its foot, but its brethren frisked about all unheeding.

Hyla saw nothing for a time. He seemed thinking. His intelligent eyes were glazed and far away, only the impassive, hairless face remained, with little or no soul to brighten it. And yet a great struggle was surging over this poor man's heart, and such as he had never known before. To his rough and animal life an emotional crisis was new and startling. Something seemed to have suddenly given way in his brain—some membrane which hitherto had separated him from real things.

While the little dog struggled and yelped as its bleeding paw was thrust in measurement through the metal ring, a new man was being born. Hyla's sub-conscious brain told him that nothing that had happened before mattered a shred of straw. He had never understood what life might mean for a man till now.

An Ideal was suddenly revealed to him. But to accept that ideal? that was hard indeed. It meant almost certain death and torture for himself.

The promptings of self-interest, which spring from our lower nature, and which are pictorially personified into a grim personality, began to flutter and whisper.

"Supposing," they said, "that you did this, that you killed Geoffroi for his sins, and to show that the down-trodden and the poor are yet men, and can exact a penalty. How much better would your companions be? Fulke would be lord then, and he is even as his father. Let it go, hold Gruach in your arms—you have that joy, you know. And work is not so bad. They have not beaten you yet; there are sometimes good things to eat and drink, are there not? Mind when you took home a whole mess of goose and garlic from the hall door? Often you snare a rabbit, and the minter is not ill-disposed to you. You are the best of his men; to you it is given to drive the die and hammer the coin, to beat the die into the silver and to burnish it. It is possible—stranger things have happened—that you might even gain freedom, and become a villein. Lewin might speak for you—who knows? These things have happened before. Is it indeed worth while to do this thing?"

While these thoughts were racing through Hyla's brain, and he was considering them, a strange thing happened. To the struggling brain of the serf, all unused to any subtle emotion, Nature made a direct æsthetic appeal.

In the middle sky a lark began to trill a song so loud and tuneful, so instinct with Freedom, that it seemed a direct message to him. He stared up at the tiny speck from which these heavenly notes were falling down to earth, and his doubts rolled up like a curtain.

He saw that it was his duty to kill Geoffroi for the sake of the others, and, come what might, he said to himself that he would do this thing.

The clumsy medium of the printed page has allowed us to follow Hyla's thoughts very slowly. Even as his resolve was taken, he heard Cerdic muttering that it was "ill to fumble with Satan's tail."

"I'll do it," he said, "and it's not the Divell that will be glad, Cerdic. No, it's not the Divell," he repeated, a little at a loss what further to say.

Cerdic pulled from his tunic a little cross of wood, and held it out to him. The passer-by would have seen two serfs, ill-clothed, unwashed, uncouth, eating bread and cheese under a wall. He would never have put a thought to them. Yet the conference of the two was fraught with tremendous meaning to those times. For a hundred years Hyla was remembered, and a star in the darkness to the weary; and after his name was forgotten, the influence of his deeds made life sweeter for many generations of the poor.

Hyla took the little cross, so that he might swear faith. With a lingering memory of the form in which men swore oath of fealty to their lords, he said, "I become true man to this deed from this day forward, of life and limb and earthly service, and unto it shall be true and faithful, and bear to you faith, Cerdic, for the aid I claim to hold of you."

He did this in seriousness, beyond all opinion; but the importance of the occasion, and the drama of it, pleased him not a little. The new toy of words was pleasant.

Cerdic kissed him, entering into the spirit of the oath, for it was the custom to kiss a man sworn to service.

"And I also am with you to the end," said Cerdic, "and may all false ribalds die who use poor men so."

In a high voice which shook with hate he quavered out a verse of the "Song of the Husbandman," a popular political song of those days; a ballad which the common people sang under their breath:

"Ne mai us nyse no rest rycheis ne ro.

Thus me pileth the pore that is of lute pris:

Nede in swot and in swynk swynde mot swo."

It was the poor fellow's Marseillaise!

"There may not arise to us, or remain with us, riches or rest. Thus they rob the poor man, who is of little value: he must waste away in sweat and labour."

Doggerel, but how bitter! A sign of the times which Geoffroi could not hear—ominous, threatening.

"A right good song, Cerdic," said Hyla. "But it will not be ever so. I know not if we shall see it, but all things change and change shall come from us. A tree stands not for ever."

The two men gazed steadfastly into each other's eyes, and then went about their work in silence.

The drama of this history may now be said to have begun. The lamps are trimmed, the scene set, and you shall hear the stirring story of Hyla the Serf.

CHAPTER III

The last night of Geoffroi de la Bourne

While Cerdic and Hyla sat in the field weaving their design to completion, Lord Geoffroi, Lord Fulke, Lady Alice, and Brian de Burgh, the squire, set out after forest game. They were attended by a great hunting train. Very few people of any importance were left in the castle, save Lewin and Dom Anselm.

The sun, though still very hot, had begun to decline towards his western bower, and the quiet of the afternoon already seemed to foreshadow the ultimate peace of evening.

Very little was doing in the castle. Some of the grooms lay about sleeping in the sun, waiting the long return of the hunters in idleness. From the armoury now and again the musical tinkering of a chisel upon steel sounded intermittent. Soon this also stopped, and a weapon-smith, who had been engraving foliates upon a blade, came out of his forge yawning. The Pantler, a little stomachy man, descended from the great hall, and, passing through the court, went out of the great gate into the village. Time seemed all standing still, in the silence and the heat.

Dom Anselm came into the courtyard, and sat him down upon a bench by the draw-well, just in the fringe of the long violet shadow thrown over the yard by Outfangthef. There was a bucket of water, full of cool green lights, standing by the well. After a little consideration, the priest kicked off his sandals and thrust his feet into its translucence. Then, comfortably propped up against the post, he fell to reading his Latin-book. In half-an-hour the book had slipped from his hand, and he was fast asleep.

While he slept, a door opened in the tower. From it came Pierce, and after him two girls, tall, comely Saxon lasses, bronzed by sun and wind. One of them, the eldest of the two, held her hands clenched, and her face was set in sullen silence. Her eyes alone blazed, and were dilated with anger. The younger girl seemed more at ease. Her eyes were timid, but a half smile lingered on her pretty, rather foolish lips. She fingered a massive bracelet of silver which encircled her arm. Pierce was giving Frija and Elgifu their freedom.

They came down the steps, and he pointed across the courtyard towards the gateway passage. "There! girls," said he, "there lies your way, to take or leave, just as suits your mind. For me, were I you, I'd never go back to the stoke. Hard fare, and dogs lying beyond all opinion! My Lords bid me say that you can take your choice."

Frija swung round at him, shaking with passion.

"Vitaille and bower," she shrilled at him, "and the prys shame! A lord for a leofman, indeed! Before I would fill my belly with lemman's food to your lord's pleasure, I would throw myself from Outfangthef."

Pierce smiled calmly at her.

"You talk of shame!—it is my lord's, if shame there is! Off with you to the fold, little serf lamb!"

She flushed a deep crimson, and seemed to cower at his words. "Come, Elgifu," she said, "mother will be glad to see us come, even coming as we do."

"Pretty Elgifu!" said the man. "No, you are not going! My Lord Fulke's a fine young man. Did he not give you that bracelet? Stay here with us all, good comrades, and you shall be our little friend. We will treat you well. Is it not so?"

The girl hesitated. She was a pretty, brainless little thing, and had not protested. They had been kind enough to her. The stoke seemed very horrible and noisome after the glories of the castle. Her sister's burning flow of Saxon seemed unnecessary. Frija looked at her in surprise at her hesitation.

"Say nothing to the divell," she cried impatiently; "come you home to mother."

Her imperious elder sister's tone irritated the little fool. "No, then," she said. "I will stay here. I will not go with you. You may talk of 'shame,' but if shame it is to live in this tower, then I have shame for my choys. Life is short; it is better here."

With that frank confession, she turned to the man-at-arms for approval.

He stepped in front of her, and, scowling at Frija, bid her be off. With a great cry of sorrow, the elder girl bowed her head and swiftly walked away. They saw her disappear through the gateway, and heard the challenge and laughter of the guards, pursuing her with jests as she went by.

"Oh, you are wise, pretty one!" said Pierce, putting his arm round her waist. "See, now, I will take you to the topmost part of the tower, to that balcony. We shall see all the country-side from there!"

The Serf

They turned and entered Outfangthef, and the clanging of the door as it closed behind them roused Anselm from his slumber.

He sat up, stupidly gazing round him. His book was fallen, and a dog was nosing in its pages. He kicked the cur away, and picked up the breviary. By the shadow of the tower, which stood at the corner of the keep, he saw the afternoon was getting on. He looked round him impatiently, and, even as he did so, saw the man he was expectant of approaching.

"I am late," said Lewin, as he came up; "but I have been hearing news, and have much to tell you. We had better go at once."

"Whiles I fetch my staff," said the other, and soon they were walking through the village, down the road which led to the fen. They came to the fields, where a herd of swine was feeding among the sewage.

"They are unclean things," said Lewin, regarding them with dislike. "Though I am no Jew in practice, yet I confess that I do not like them. Pig! the very name is an outrage to one's ear."

"So not I," said Dom Anselm. "When the brute lives in the charge of a Saxon slave, she goes by her Saxon name; but she becomes a Norman, and is called 'pork,' when she is carried to castle-hall to feast among us. I want no better dish."

"Each to his taste. But here we are. By the Mass, but the place stinks!"

They had come to the landing-stage in the river, and, indeed, the odour was almost unbearable. For twenty yards round, the water was thick with foulness. They got into a flat-bottomed boat and pushed off across the stream. The water was too deep to pole in the centre, but one or two vigorous strokes sent them gliding towards the further rushes. Lewin punted skilfully, skirting the reeds, which rose far above his head, until he came to a narrow opening.

"This will do as well as another," he said, and turned the boat down it.

The water-way was little more than two yards wide, and the reeds grew thick and high, so that they could only see a little way in front. At last, after many turns and twists, they came to a still, green pool, a hundred yards across. In this stagnant evil-looking place they rested, floating motionless in the centre.

"Geoffroi himself, were he in the reeds, could not hear us now," said the priest.

"True, but drop a line to give a reason for being here."

The priest took from his girdle a line, wound upon a wooden spool. Baiting the hook with a piece of meat, he dropped it overboard, and settled himself comfortably in the bottom of the boat.

"Now, Lewin," said he, "you may go into the matter."

"I will tell you all I have heard," said the minter, "and we will settle all we purpose to do. You have heard that Roger Bigot has taken Norwich, and assumed the earldom of the county in rebellion to the king. Hamo de Copton, the moneyer, is a correspondent of mine, from London, and we have been interested together in more than one mercantile venture. From him letters are to hand upon the disposal of four chests of silver triens in London. You know our money is but token money, and not worth the face value of the stamp. We are making trial to circulate our money through Hamo, and in return he sends Lord Geoffroi bars of silver uncoined. Now, the letter bears a post scriptum to this end. 'The king is sick, and indeed was taken so before Whitsuntide.' The talk is all that his cause is losing, and that wise men will be nimble to seize opportunity. Hamo urges me to consider well if I should seek some other master than Geoffroi, who is the king's friend."

He stopped suddenly, alarmed by a great disturbance in the water. A pike had swallowed Anselm's bait and was beating about the pool five or six yards away, leaping out of the water in its agony. They hauled the line in slowly, until the great, evil-looking creature was snapping and writhing at the boatside. Then, with a joint heave, it lay at the bottom of the boat, and was soon despatched by the minter's dagger.

"Go on," said Dom Anselm.

"Yestreen," resumed Lewin, "John Heyrown was privy with me for near two hours. He comes peddling spice from Dentown, hard by Norwich town. I have known him privily these six months. From him I hear that Roger Bigot is in the article of setting forth to come upon us here to take the castle. Geoffroi has great store of fine armour of war, eke fine metals and jewels of silver and gold. Hilgay would extend Roger's arm far south, and make a fort for him on the eastern road to London. He is pressing to London with a great force and inventions of war. Now, listen, John Heyrown is neither more nor less than in his pay, and he comes here to see if he can find friends within our walls. Roger knows of me and my value, and offereth me a high place, and also for my friends, do I but help him. What do you say?"

Dom Anselm's thin face wrinkled up in thought, weighing the chances.

"I think," he said at last, very slowly, "I think, that we must throw our lot in with Roger Bigot, and be his men."

"I also," said Lewin. "And I have already been preparing a token of our choice."

He pulled a piece of vellum from his tunic.

"Here is a map of the castle, clear drawn. There you see marked the weak spot by the orchard wall; Geoffroi has been long a-mending of it since we noticed the sinking, but nothing has been done. To enter the castle need not be difficult. The donjon will be harder; but I have marked a plan for that also. At the foot of Outfangthef lie *les oubliettes*, and many deep cellars, raised on arches. It is there keep we our coined silver and the silver in bars. With his engines, knowing the spot, Roger could mine deep, and Outfangthef would fall, leaving a great breach."

Anselm took the plan with admiration.

"It's finely writ," he said; "should'st have been in a scriptorium."

"My two hands are good thralls to me," said Lewin, pleased at the compliment to his work. "Then you and I stand committed to this thing?"

"Since it seems the wisest course, for Lord Roger is a great lord and strong, I give you my hand."

"Let it be so, friend Anselm. I will give John the plan this night."

"Then it is a thing done. But what is your immediate end?—for I conceive you have some near purpose in view."

"Some time I will tell you, but not yet."

"It's a woman, you dog!" said the priest with a grin.

"We must homewards," answered the other. "Hark! I hear the horns, they have returned from the chase."

As he spoke, clear and sweet the tantivy came floating down the hill and over the water.

"We shall be late for supper," said Lewin, "make haste; take the other pole."

"God forbid we should be late for supper," said Anselm, and they began to push back.

"Will Geoffroi know that Roger is about to attack Hilgay?" Anselm asked Lewin.

"Certainly he will, in a day or two. You may be sure that he has friends in Norwich, and an expedition does not start without a clatter and talk all along the country-side. I would wager you a wager, Sir Anselm, that Geoffroi will hear of it by to-morrow morn."

"And then?"

"Why then to making ready, to get provision and vitaille for the siege."

"Well, I wait it in patience: I never moil and fret. He who waiteth, all things reach at the last."

"Beware of too much patience, Sir Anselm. Mind you the fable of Chiche Vache, the monstrous cow, who fed entirely on patient men and women, and, the tale went, was sorely lean on that fare?

"'Gardez vous de la shicheface,

El vous mordra s'el vous encontre.'"

The Jew gave out the song with a fine trill in his voice, which was as tuneful as a bell.

The priest, as he watched him and marked his handsome, intelligent face, was filled with wonder of him. There was nothing he could not do well, so ran his thoughts, and an air of accomplishment and ease was attendant upon all his movements. As he threw back his head, drinking in the evening air, and humming his catch—"el vous mordra s'el vous encontre"—Anselm was suddenly filled with fear of him. He seemed not quite to fit into life. He was a Jew, too, and his forefathers had scourged God Incarnate. Strange things were said about the Jews—art magic helped them in their work. The priest clutched the cross by his side, and there was a wonderful comfort in the mere physical contact with it.

"No," said he, "I have never heard of Chiche Vache that I can call to mind. I do not care much for fables and fairy tales. There is merry reading in the lives of Saints, and good for the soul withal."

"The loss is yours, priest. I love the stories and tales of the common folk, eke the songs they sing to the children. I can learn much from them. Chiche Vache is as common to the English as to French folk. 'Lest Chichewache yow swelwe in hir entraille,'" he drawled in a capital imitation of the uncouth Saxon speech.

By that time they had got to the castle and turned in at its gates.

The courtyard was full with a press of people, and busy as a hive. Outside the stable doors the horses were being rubbed down by the serfs. As they splashed the cool water over the quivering fetlocks and hot legs, all scratched by thorns and forest growth, they crooned a little song in unison. The "ballad of my lord going hawking" was a melancholy cadence, which seemed, in its slow minors, instinct with the sadness of a conquered race. The first verse ran—

"Lord his wyfe upstood and kyssed,

Faucon peregryn on wryst;

Faucon she of fremde londe,

With hir beek Sir Heyrown fonde."

Lewin and Anselm passed by them and stood watching a moment.

"Hear you that song of the grooms?" Lewin said.

"I have heard it a hundred times, but never listened till now," said Anselm. "But what say they of Faucon peregryn? what means fremde londe?"

"It stands for foreign land in their speech," said the Jew. "Hast much to learn of thy flock, Anselm?"

"Not I. My belly moves at the crooning. It is like the wind in the forest of a winter's night. Come you to supper."

"That I will, when I have washed my hands; they are all foul with pike's blood."

Dom Anselm gave a superior smile, and turned towards the hall.

The Serf

The great keep lifted its huge angular block of masonry high into the ruddy evening air, Outfangthef frowned over the bailey below. The door which opened on the hall steps stood wide, and the servants were hurrying in and out with dishes of food, while the men-at-arms stood lingering round it till supper should be ready.

Cookery was an art upon the upward path, and Geoffroi's *chef* was no mean professor of it. The hungry crowd saw bowls of stew made from goose and garlic borne up the stairs. Pork and venison in great quarters followed, and after them came two kitchen serfs carrying wooden trays of pastry, and round cakes piously marked with a cross.

Soon came the summons to supper. A page boy came down the steps and cried that my lord was seated, and every one pressed up the stairs with much jangling of metal and grinding of feet upon the stones. To our modern ideas the great hall would present an extraordinary sight. This rich nobleman fed with less outward-seeming comfort than a pauper in a clean-scrubbed, whitewashed workhouse of to-day. And yet, though many a lazy casual would grumble at a dinner served as was Geoffroi de la Bourne's, there was something enormously impressive in the scene. We are fortunate in many old chronicles and tales which enable us to reconstruct it in all its picturesqueness.

Imagine, then, that you are standing on the threshold of the hall just as supper has been begun.

The hall was a great room of bare stone, with a roof of oaken beams, in which more than one bird had its nest. There was an enormous stone chimney, now all empty of fire, and the place was lit with narrow chinks, unglazed, pierced in the ten-foot wall. The day of splendid oriels was yet to come in fortress architecture, which was, like the time, grim and stern. It was dusk now in the outside world, and the hall was lit with horn lanterns, and also with tall spiked sticks, into which were fixed rough candles of tallow. The table went right up the hall, and was a heavy board supported on trestles. Benches were the only seats.

On a daïs at the far end of the building was the high table, where Geoffroi and his son and daughter sat. The two squires, Brian de Burgh and Richard Ferville, also sat at the high table, and Dom Anselm had a place on the baron's right hand.

Lewin was seated at the head of the lower table, and the baron could lean over and speak to him if he had a mind to do so.

Geoffroi and his son sat in chairs which were covered with rugs, and at their side stood great goblets of silver. The dim light threw fantastic shadows upon the colours of the dresses and the weapons hung on pegs driven into the wall, blending them into a harmonious whole.

It was a picture of warm reds and browns, of mellow, comfortable colours, with here and there a sudden twinkle of rich, vivid madder or old gold.

When every one was seated, Geoffroi nodded to Dom Anselm, who thereupon pattered out a grace, an act of devotion which was rather marred by the behaviour of Lord Fulke, who was audibly relating some merry tale to his friend, Brian de Burgh.

Then every one fell to with a great appetite. The serfs, kneeling, brought barons of beef and quarters of hot pork on iron dishes. Each man cut what he fancied with his dagger or hunting-knife, and laid it on his trencher. Such as chose stew or ragout, ate it from a wooden bowl, scooping up the mess in their bare hands. Lady Alice held a bone in her white fingers, and gnawed it like any kitchen wench; and so did they all, and were, indeed, none the worse for that.

Geoffroi de la Bourne, the central figure of that company, was a tall, thin man of some five-and-fifty years. His face was lined and seamed with deep furrows. Heavy brows hung over cold green eyes, and a beaked eagle nose dominated a small grey moustache, which did not hide a pair of firm, thin lips. His grey hair fell almost to his shoulders.

The Serf

Geoffroi, like his son and the squires, was dressed in a tunic, long, tight hose, a short cloak trimmed with expensive fur, and shoes with peaked corkscrew toes.

The Baron sat eating quickly, and joining little in the talk around him. He seemed very conscious of his position as lord of vast lands, and had the exaggerated manner of the overworked business man.

He had many things to trouble him. The mint was not going well. His unblushing adulteration of coined monies was severely commented on, and his silver pennies were looked upon with suspicion in more than one mercantile centre. The king was ill, and the license made possible by the disordered state of the country was exciting the great churchmen to every intrigue against the barons. Moreover, plunder was become increasingly difficult. Merchants no longer passed with their trains anywhere near the notorious castle of Hilgay, and, except for his immediate retainers, all the country round was up in arms against Geoffroi.

He had imagined that stern, repressive measures would terrify his less powerful neighbours into silence. Two flaming churches in the fens and the summary hanging of the priests had, however, only incensed East Anglia to a passion of hatred.

Even as he sat at supper a certain popular Saxon gentleman, Byrlitelm by name, lay at the bottom of an unmentionable hole beneath Outfangthef, groaning his life away in darkness and silence, while his daughter was the sport and plaything of the two young squires. Disquieting rumours were abroad about the intentions of the powerful Roger Bigot of Norwich, who was known to be hand-in-glove with the Earl of Gloucester, the half-brother of Matilda.

Added to these weighty troubles, Geoffroi, who like all nobles of that day was an expert carver in wood and metal, had cut his thumb almost to the bone by the slip of a graving tool, and it throbbed unbearably. A still further annoyance threatened him. Gertrude of Albermarl, a little girl of fifteen, now acting as an attendant to Lady Alice, was a ward of his whom he had taken quietly, usurping one of the especial privileges of his friend the king.

The Crown managed the estates of minors, and held the right of giving in marriage the heirs and heiresses of its tenants. "The poor child may be tossed and tumbled chopped and changed, bought and sold, like a jade in Smithfield, and, what is more, married to whom it pleaseth his guardian—whereof many evils ensue," says Jocelyn de Brakelond, and the wardship of little Gertrude was a very comfortable thing. Stephen had heard of this act of Geoffroi's, and had sent him a peremptory summons to send the child immediately to town. Geoffroi had that day determined that little Gertrude should be married incontinently, to the young ruffian his son, but the step was a grave one to take, and would probably alienate the king irrevocably.

So he ate his supper gloomily. Every one in the place knew immediately that he was displeased, and it cast a gloom over them also.

As the meal went on, conversation became fitful and constrained, and the crowd of lecheurs, or beggars, who waited round the door, disputing scraps of food with the lean fen dogs, could be distinctly heard growling and gobbling among themselves in obscene chatter.

When at last Lady Alice withdrew and the cups were filled afresh with cool wine from the cellar, Geoffroi signed to Fulke to come up to him. The young man was a debauched creature of twenty-six, clean-shaven. His hair was not long like his father's, but clipped close. The back of his head was also shaven, and gave him a fantastic, elfin appearance. It was a custom to shave the back of the head, which was very generally adopted, especially in hot weather, among the young dandies of the time.

It is quite possible that this fashion of the shavelings accounted for the mistake of Harold's spies at the Conquest, who said that there were more priests in the Norman camp than fighting men in the English army!

"Letters from the king," said Geoffroi shortly, in a deep, hoarse voice.

"About Gertrude?"

"Yes, that is it. Now there is but one answer to make to that. You must marry her in a day or so, and then nothing more can be said."

"That is the only thing," said Fulke, grinning and wrinkling up his forehead till his stubble of hair seemed squirting out of it. "But I will not give up my pleasures for that."

"Who asked you?" said the father. "She is but a child and a-knoweth nothing—you can make them her maids-in-waiting, that will please her." He laughed a short, snarling laugh. "Sir Anselm shall tie the knot with Holy Church her benediction."

He summoned that scandalous old person from his wine.

"Priest," said he, "my Lord Fulke is about to wed little Lady Gertrude; so make you ready in a day or two. I will give you the gold cross I took from Medhampstede, for a memorial, and we will eke have a feast for every one of my people."

"It is the wisest possible thing, Lord Geoffroi," said Anselm. "I will say a Mass or two and get to praying for the young folk, and Heaven will be kind to them."

"That do," said Fulke and Geoffroi, making the sign of the cross, for, strange as it may seem, both the scoundrels were real believers in the mysterious powers of the chaplain. Though they saw him drunken, lecherous, and foul of tongue, yet they believed entirely in his power to arrange things for them with God. Indeed, paradoxical as it may sound, if Anselm had not been at Hilgay, both of them would have been better men. They would not have dared some of their excesses, had it not been possible to obtain immediate absolution. A rape and a murder were cheap at a pound of wax altar lights and a special Mass.

"Here's good fortune," said Anselm, lifting the cup and bowing to Fulke.

"Thank you for't," said the young man. "Father, the minter shall make us a ring, and his mouth shall give the tidings to the other officers. Lewin, come you here, you have a health to drink." Lewin was summoned to the upper table, and sat drinking with them, pledging many toasts. Once he cast a curious glance at Anselm, and that worthy smiled back at him.

The evening was growing very hot and oppressive as it wore on. It was quite dark outside and there was thunder in the air. Every now and again the sky muttered in wrath, and at such sounds a sudden stillness fell upon the four knaves at the high table, and, putting down their wine vessels, they crossed themselves. Lewin made the "great cross" each time, "from brow to navel, and from arm to arm."

Little Gertrude was long since a-bed, her prayers said, and her little dark head tucked under the coverlet. She felt quite safe from the thunder, for she had invoked Saint Peter, Saint Paul, Saint Luke and Saint Matthew, to stand round her bed all night, and she knew that they would be there while she slept. Who, indeed, shall say that my Lords the Saints were not guarding the sleeping child on that eventful night?

Geoffroi began to be less taciturn as the wine warmed him. Some bone dice were produced, and they fell to playing for silver pennies. One of the squires joined them, but the other left the hall early, as he had some tender business afoot with Gundruda, the pretty serving-maid.

In the middle of the game, a stir came about at the hall door. One or two of the soldiers went to see what was toward. A traveller, wet with rain, was asking speech with Geoffroi, and he was brought up to the high table by Huber and John.

"My lord," said he, "you will remember me. I am Oswald, your liege man. I come from Norwich bearing news of war. I have been there a-buying rams, and I bring you grave news. Roger Bigot is arming all his men in hot speed, and comes to Hilgay to overthrow us. In a week or two he will be here. He is very strong in arms."

These tidings affected the five men very differently.

Lewin glanced quickly at Anselm, and then turned to Oswald, waiting more. The young squire tossed his head, and rang his hand upon the table joyously. Fulke's lips tightened, and an ugly light came into his eyes. The Baron alone showed no outward sign of agitation. He drummed his fingers on the side of the wine-goblet for a minute, in silence.

Then he suddenly looked up, "Well," he said, "that is news, Oswald, but I had thought to hear it a month since! Let the man come up against me if he will, he shall rot for't, damn his soul! I am lord of this country-side, with a rare lot of devils, lusty for blood, to guard this keep. A week, you say? Very well, in a week he shall find us ready. But get you to the table, Oswald, along of my merry men, and see that you drink in God's name. Get you drunken, Oswald, my man; I thank you for this. Get you drunk. Really, you should, in God's name. Huber! John! Tell Master Pantler from me to put rope to windlass and draw up a cask of wine for the men-at-arms. Hei! Hei!! Hei!!!" he shouted in a vast and wonderful voice, rising in his seat and holding his beaker above his head, "Men of mine! men of mine! my Lord Roger Bigot, the bastard from Norwich town, lusteth for our blood and castle. The foining scamp a-comes riding with a great force to take us. Drink ye all to me, men of mine, and we will go against this traitor to the king—Hei! Hei! Hei!"

There was a fierce roar of exultation which pierced the very roof. The war spirit ran like fire round the great hall, and as Geoffroi's tall figure stood high above them, his voice rolled louder than the mightest shouter there.

They broached the cask of wine, and brought torches into the hall until the whole place flamed with light. The enthusiasm was indescribable. They had all been long spoiling for a fight, and here was news indeed! Oswald was plied with drink and pestered with questions.

When, in some half-hour's time, the excitement had in some degree subsided, it began to be told among the men that a jongleur was in the castle, and had been there since the afternoon. Lewin told Geoffroi of this, and the man was sent for, so that he might amuse them with songs of battle.

CHAPTER IV

Other incidents which occurred on the last night of Geoffroi de la Bourne

In the early Middle Ages, no less than now, men and women believed in ominous happenings to those about to die. Strange things were known to occur in monasteries when a priest was going, and it was said that the night before a battle soldiers would sometimes feel an icy cold wind upon their faces, which fell from Death himself, beating his great wings.

There were no materialists in England in those times, and the unseen world was very near and present to men's minds.

On this night of thunder and alarms, there was to happen another of those supernatural occurrences which are so difficult to explain away.

About the time the jongleur was brought into the hall—a little elderly man, very pleasant and merry, but yet with something greedy, brutal, and dangerous in his face—the

The Serf

enclosure of the serfs began to be agitated by new and terrible emotions. Tragedy, indeed, had often entered there, but it was at the bidding of some one in the outside world. To-night she was to be invoked by the down-trodden and oppressed themselves.

When men are gathered together, set upon some fearful act of retribution or revenge, the very air seems instinct with the thoughts that are in their hearts, and fluid with the electricity of the great deed to be done.

In the centre of the stoke the common fire burnt without flame, for the rain had tamed it. Round the fire sat the conspirators, and in the stillness, for the rain was over and there was no wind, the murmuring of their voice seemed like the note of an organ hidden in the wood.

Round the stoke the giant trees made a tremendous sable wall, grim and silent, and even the dark sky above was brighter and more hopeful than the silent company of trees. The sky was full of flickering lightnings—white, green, and amethyst—and ever and again the thunder murmured from somewhere over against Ely. Sometimes a spear of lightning came right into the stoke, cracking like a whip.

The little group of inky figures round the embers seemed in no way disturbed by the elements, but only drew closer and fell into more earnest talk.

Hyla, Cerdic, Harl, Gurth, and Richard, sat planning the murder of Geoffroi. On the morrow the Baron was to ride after a great boar which the foresters knew of in the wood. This was settled, and it was thought there would be a great hunt, for the boar was cunning, fierce, and old.

Now Geoffroi was skilled in all the elaborate science of woodcraft. He knew every word of the pedantic Norman jargon of the hunt in all its extravagance. He could wind upon his horn every mot known to the chase, and no man could use the dissecting dagger upon a dead stag more scientifically than he. More than all this, he rode better and with more ardour than either his son or squires. Often it would happen that he would gallop far into the forest after game, outstripping all his train. They were used to that, and would often start another quarry for themselves. Geoffroi was a moody man, happy alone, privy to himself, and it had become somewhat of a custom to let him ride alone.

Now the serfs plotted that they should lie hidden in the underwood and turn the boar towards a distant glade called Monkshood. In that open space—for the trees were sparse there and studded the turf at wide intervals—it was probable that Geoffroi would wind the death mot of the quarry. It was to be his last mellow call in this world, for Hyla planned to take him as he stood over the dead boar and kill him in the ride.

Then when he had done the work, he was to return through the brushwood towards the village. Provided only that the other hunters were far away while he was killing the Baron, his presence in the wood would excite little comment, even if he was seen returning. Moreover, he purposed to carry an armful of dry sticks, so that he might appear as if he were gathering kindling wood.

He would reach the stoke, he thought, just about the time that the huntsmen would discover the Baron lying stark. He was to go through the village, down the hill to the river, and embark in a small punt. He would fly for his life then, poling swiftly through all the water-ways of the fen till he reached Icombe in the heart of the waters, where he should find sanctuary and lie hid till happier times.

Hyla sat among them curiously confident. He never for a moment doubted the result of the enterprise. None of them did. The resolution which they had taken was too overwhelming to allow a suspicion of failure.

There was something terrible in this grim certainty.

The Serf

In an hour or two, Gruach and Frija, with the two little prattling boys, were to be taken down to the river and to set out for the Priory beforehand, so that Hyla should find them waiting him. Harl was to punt throughout the night, hoping to reach safety by dawn. It was a hard journey, for the Priory was fifteen miles away.

"It is near time to set out," said Harl. "My heart is gride at this night's work."

"Sore things always happen in time of wracke," said Cerdic. "See that you protect Gruach and Frija in their unlustiness."

"The boat shall speed as boat never did before, and they shall be safe at dawning."

Hyla had been sitting in silence staring at the red heart of the fire as if he saw pictures there. "I am nothing accoyed," he said at length, "I fear nothing save for Elgifu."

Harl beat upon the ground with his fist. "An you kill Geoffroi, I have a mind to deal with Fulke also in sic a way. Little Elgifu!"

"She was always a little fool," said Hyla roughly. "She has made choys and lies in the arms of a lord. Think no more of her, Harl. I hope they will not hurt her, that is all."

"They will not hurt her, I wote," Cerdic broke in cheerfully. "They will gain nothing by that. She is a piece of goods of value. They will not hurt her."

The arrangements were all made for the flight of Gruach and Frija; the plot was planned in every detail, and a silence fell upon them. Few of them had the art of conversation or knew how to talk. Hyla sat silent, with nothing in his brain to say. Although he was in a state of fierce excitement, of exultation at a revelation of self, which appeared miraculous in its freshness—as if he had been suddenly given a new personality—he had never a word to say. Cerdic was his firm and faithful friend, but he could express none of the thoughts surging over him even to Cerdic. The poor toiling, tired souls had never learnt the gift of speech; they were cut off from each other, except in the rarest instances.

For example, a combination, such as the one we are discussing, was unheard of. Of course, only a few of the serfs had been told of the plot, for it would not have been safe in the hands of many of them. Yet, that eight or nine men, with all the stumbling blocks of inherited slavery, a miserable life, and an incredible lack of opportunity, should have learnt and put in practice the lesson of combination, is a most startling fact.

"Combination," indeed, was born that night, and stood ready to be clothed with a vigorous life, and to supply the means for a slow but glorious revolution. The direct effects of the proceedings at Hilgay have affected our whole history to this day.

After a half-hour of silence, broken only by an occasional word-of-course, the women, who had been sleeping to gain strength, were summoned for departure.

The great enterprise seemed to knit the men at the fire together in a wonderful way. They felt they must keep with each other, and all rose to accompany the fugitives to the river. The little boys, sleepily protesting, were carried in the arms of two of the men, and the melancholy procession stole out into the warm darkness. The other serfs were all asleep, and deep breathings resounded as they passed the huts. At the entrance to the stoke a mongrel dog barked at them, but a blow with a stick sent him away whining.

In a few minutes, treading very quietly, they were passing along the green by the castle. There were still points of light in the towering black walls, and distant sounds of revelry coming to them sent them along with faster steps.

Now that the enterprise was actually embarked upon, most of them felt very uneasy. The mere sight of that enormous pile brought before their minds the tremendous power they were going up against. It was so visible and tangible a thing, such a symbol of their own poor estate.

But Frija, as she passed the castle, spat towards the palisades and ground her teeth in fury. That heartened them up a little. They had wives and daughters also. As Gruach passed, she wept bitterly for Elgifu within. They went without mishap through the village. All the houses were silent and showed no sign of life. The way was very dark, though the white chalk of the road helped them a little to find it. Also, now and then, the lightning lit up the scene strangely, showing the members of the group to each other, hurrying, very furtive and white of face.

The fens opened before them as a wall of white vapour. No stranger would have imagined the vast flat expanses beyond. The mist might have concealed any other kind of scenery. Standing on the hill they could see the mysterious blue lights dancing over the fen. They crossed themselves at that. It was thought that restless souls danced over the waters at night, and that many evil things were abroad after dark.

They were quite close to the landing-stage and, encircled by the mist, walking very warily, when Harl, who was a pioneer, was heard to give a quick shout of alarm.

Another voice was heard roughly challenging. They passed through the vapour and came suddenly upon Pierce, the man-at-arms. At his feet lay a heap of fish, phosphorescent in the dark. He looked at them with deep amazement. "What are you?" he said.

As he spoke, and his voice gave clue to his identity, Hyla gathered himself together and leapt upon him. The two men fell with a great clatter on to the very edge of the landing-stage, slipping and struggling among the great heap of wet fish. Had not the others come to their assistance both would have been in the water.

Hyla rose bleeding from scratches on the face. Gurth had a great bony hand over the soldier's mouth, and the others held him pinned to the ground, so that he was quite powerless.

"Get the women away," said Cerdic, "get the women away."

Harl stepped from punt to punt until he came to a long light boat of oak, low in the water, and built for speed. He cast off the rope which tied it to one of the other punts, and brought it alongside the steps. He put a bundle of clothing and food in the centre, and waited for Gruach and her daughter.

Hyla lifted the little boys, wrapped in cat-skins, into the boat, and turned to Gruach. She lay sobbing in his arms, pressing her wet face to his.

"Pray Lord Christ that I am with you on the morrow, wife," he said, "and fare you well!" He embraced Frija, and helped both women into the boat. Harl took up the pole.

"Farewell!" came in a deep, low chorus from the group of serfs, and, with no further words, the boat shot away into the dark. They could hear the splash of the pole and the wailing of the women, and then the darkness closed up and hid them utterly.

The men closed round Pierce. There seemed no hesitation in their movements. It was felt by every one that he must die. Despite his frantic struggles, they unbuckled his belt and dagger. Cerdic pulled down the neck of his tunic and laid bare the flesh beneath. Hyla unsheathed the dagger, trembling with joy as his enemy lay beneath him——

It was as easy as killing a cat, and they took the body and sank it in mid-stream. Then they stood upon the landing-stage speechless, huddled close together—torn by exultation and fear.

Cerdic saw that they were terrified at what had been done. "Come, friends," said he, "fall upon your knees with me, and pray the Blessed Virgin to shed her favour upon Hyla and his work to-morrow. The fish are at one black knave already, to-morrow a greater shall meet his man in hell. Our Lady and my Lords the Saints are with us; get you to praying."

The Serf

In a moment a sudden flash of lightning, which leapt across the great arch of heaven, showed a group of kneeling forms, silent, with bended heads.

Soon they went stealing up the hill again, but not before Gurth had delivered himself of a grim, though practical pleasantry. "I'll have the divell's fish," he said, and with that he slung them over his shoulder, for they were threaded upon a string.

The jongleur in the hall played upon his crowth, and sang them Serventes, Lays, and songs of battle. Between each song he rested his fiddle upon the floor and drank a draught of morat, till his lips and chin were all purple with the mulberry juice. Then he would say that he would give them a little something which dealt with the great surquedy and outrecuidance of a certain baron, the son of a lady of ill-fame, and how, being in his cups, this man was minded to go up in fight against a rock. So, forthwith, the hero got him up on his destrier and ran full tilt against the rock. "Then," the jongleur would conclude in quite the approved modern music-hall style, "the sward was all besprent with what remained." Vulgar wit then was own brother to coarse wit to-day, and a vulgar fool in the twelfth century differed but little from a vulgar fool in the nineteenth.

A broad grin sat solid upon the faces of the soldiers. When the jongleur began to sing little catches in couplets, plucking the string of his crowth the while for accompaniment, they nudged each other with delight at each coarse suggestion. They were exactly like a group of little foolish boys in the fourth form of a public school, just initiated into the newness of cheap wit, whispering ancient rhymes to each other.

Perhaps there was not much harm in it. When we grow to the handling of our own brain unadorned vulgarity revolts us, as a rule, but there is hardly a man, before his brain has ripened, who has not sniggered upon occasion at unpleasant trivialities. It is no manner of use ignoring the fact. Put the question to yourself, if you are a man, and remember, not without gratitude for the present, what an unprofitable little beast you were.

They were children, these men-at-arms. They had the cruelty of wolves—or children, the light-heartedness of children. Imagine what Society would be if children of fourteen were as strong and powerful as their elders. If you can conceive that, you can get a little nearer to the men-at-arms.

But as the grotesque little man mouthed and chattered, his teeth flashing white in his purple-stained jaws, like some ape, the more powerful brains at the high table had no excuse for their laughter.

The hedge priest roared with delight, Fulke sniggered meaningly, and a sardonic grin lit up the stern countenance of Geoffroi de la Bourne. Lewin must be given credit for a finer attitude. He seemed insufferably bored by the whole thing, and longing to be in bed.

The night wore on, and they drank deep, till more than one head lay low. Geoffroi filled his cup again and again, but each potation left him clearer in brain, affecting him not at all. At last he rose to seek his couch. Dom Anselm was snoring heavily, Lewin had already departed, and Fulke was playing dice with the squire.

"I have no mind to sleep for a while," Geoffroi said, "the night is hot. Bring a torch," he said to a serf; and then turning to the jongleur, "come with me, Sir Jester, to my bed-side, and relate to me some merry tales till I fall upon sleep, for I am like to wake long this night."

Preceded by the flickering of the torch, and followed by the minstrel, he left the hall. They descended the steps in red light and deepest shadow, and came out into the courtyard which was very still. Every one was asleep save one lean dog, who, hearing footsteps, padded up and thrust his cold nose into Geoffroi's hand. He fondled the

The Serf

creature, standing still for a moment, sending a keen eye round the big empty space, as who should find some enemy lurking there. The two others waited his pleasure.

"Come, come," he said at length in curiously detached tones, extremely and noticeably unlike his usual quick incisiveness, "we will get to bed."

He turned towards Outfangthef. They had taken some three paces towards the tower, when a lightning flash of dazzling brilliancy leapt right over the sky from pole to pole, and showed the whole scene as bright as in the day. Geoffroi stopped suddenly, as did the others, expecting a great peal of thunder. Suddenly the Baron began to shiver and bend. He wheeled round tottering, and caught the minstrel by the shoulder. The little man squeaked like a rat in the jaws of a dog.

"Hist!" said Geoffroi, "What do you hear? What do you hear, man?"

"Nothing, my lord," said the jongleur in deep amazement.

"Listen, jongleur. What do you hear now?" said he.

"My lord, I can hear nothing," answered the little man.

"I have drunken too deep," said the Baron; "surely I am most devilishly drunk, for I can hear, I can hear"—he leant in the manner of a man listening—"I can hear now as I speak to you, voices as of a great company of men praying to Our Lady—listen! their voices are praying deeply. I think they must be monks."

"Lord, look you to this," whispered the serf, terror-stricken.

The dog, perhaps because he felt the three men were going in fear, or perhaps from some deeper and more hidden reason which men do not yet understand, crouched low on the ground and hid his head between his paws, whining.

"They are praying to the Blessed Virgin," said Geoffroi. "Can you hear nothing—those deep voices?"

"My lord," said the jongleur with more confidence, "the night is late, and I have known many sounds appear like human voices in the night. A cow loweth or a beetle boometh in the orchard flowers."

"What it may be I do not know," answered he, "but I know that it is no ox a-lowing or fly upon the wing. I am not mocked. There is something wrong with the night."

"The more reason, Sir Geoffroi, that I should divert you with tales and jests. These fearful nights of strange lights in the sky and noises from the fen lands need some light business to fill the mind. To bed, my lord!"

"Come then," said Geoffroi. "God shield us, it is very hot," and as he turned, the sweat stood in great drops upon his brow.

At the exact moment the little party entered the door of Outfangthef, the serfs, far down in the fen, rose from their knees, and began to steal swiftly and noiselessly up the hill.

The Baron's sleeping chamber was an octagonal stone room with a groined roof. A faldestol, the great-grandfather of our own armchair, spread with cushions, stood by a tall candlestick. The bed boasted curtains and a roof, though its occupant lay upon nothing more luxurious than straw. On a low table near the faldestol were some vessels of glass and silver. Arms hung upon the walls, and a litter of shavings on the floor showed the Baron had been carving at some time during the day. On the perch by the bed head sat Geoffroi's favourite hawk, now sunk in motionless and sinister sleep.

Taken as a whole, the apartment was extremely comfortable and even luxurious in its appearance. To reconstruct it nowadays would cost the modern æsthete an enormous sum of money.

The Serf

The serf knelt at the threshold and delivered the torch to the jongleur, who lit the candle from it. Then Geoffroi shut the door, and, removing his tunic and short cloak, flung himself on the bed.

"Sit there," he said to the man, pointing to the faldestol. "There is wine upon the table if you are thirsty." Then he added with a change of manner, "you are well found in faëry tales and sic like. What means the noise I have heard to-night?"

"They say, my lord, that souls that cannot rest may be heard singing and wailing in the fen, calling on each other in reproach."

"The pot upbraiding the kettle for the soot on't! Well, well, that sweet morat is bad for a man, I think. Better stick to wine. The honey makes the brain mad."

"There is poison in many flowers," said the jongleur, "and what likes a bee's belly well enough may be bad for a man. It was the drink in you, my lord, for I heard no sound."

"It does not matter much. It is done and over. For the minute I was accoyed. Tell me a story."

"The night before the great fight of Senlac," said the jongleur, "is told of as a most wonderful strange night. The minstrel, Taillefer, went a-wandering round the camp fires, cheering the hearts of the soldiers with songs, by the order of Duke William himself. The Duke had made order that but little wine was to be given to the troops, and that they were to ride into battle shriven and fasting. So he sent Taillefer to cheer them with songs. The minstrel wandered from fire to fire over the hill till he was weary and would sleep. He came, as he went, to the old fort of the Haestingas, and there, under a ruined wall, he laid him down.

"Now my lord, Sir Taillefer was a very evil man. By the rood, but he was an evil man! Whatever deviltry a could lay his mind to, that did he, and he was in great favour with the Duke.

"Now two days before the battle the Norman army had come sailing from Saint Valeri, and had landed on the sands of England at Bulverhithe, near Pevensey, or Anderida, as some will have it. No Saxon came to oppose the landing, for the fighting men were all at the northern war on Derwent banks. In the village, Taillefer came upon a farmhouse, where the farmer was away at the war, for all the houses were empty of men. There did he find and ill-use a beautiful Saxon girl, who did resist him with many tears. He was a gay fellow, with ever a song in's mouth, but for all that, his dwelling that night was besprent with tears and wailing.

"Now, as Taillefer lay a-sleeping in the old fort, there came to him and stood by his side a long, thin man, with yellow hair and a cleft lip. 'What are you?' said Taillefer. 'Look well at me,' said the man, 'for I am the father of Githa, whom you used with violence. To-morrow morn we shall meet again. You will be singing your last song.'

"Now Taillefer was a brave man, and loved a fight, so with that he got him his axe and cleft the man from head to toe. But the blow went through the air as if no one was there, and the axe, falling upon a rock, was splintered into pieces and Taillefer a top of it, sprawling face down, and, they say, bawling most lustily. Two soldiers found him, and he said he was drunk to them, though he was no more drunk than my crowth.

"On the morrow, at nine of the clock, the bugles rang out mots of war, and the Normans were about advancing. Taillefer, in great inward fear, for he knew that he would die that day, prayed a boon from the Duke, that he might strike the first blow of the fight. He did not want to live long with the fear upon him. The Duke said aye to his question, so a-got on his destrier, and went riding out of the lines singing gaily, though 'twas said his face was very pale. He couched his lance at a Saxon, and pierced him through. Then a tall, thin man, with yellow hair and s cleft lip, came swiftly at him with a sword, and thrust it into his belly before he could recover the lance. 'It is you, then,' said Taillefer, and died in great torment."

His voice sank into silence, and he lifted the wine-cup for refreshment.

"It is a strange story," said Geoffroi, "and a pitiful to-do about a theow girl. I do not believe that story."

"I spun it as 'twas told to me, my lord," said the teller humbly.

The big man moved among the crackling straw and crossed himself, and we who have no great crime upon our conscience need not be careful to enquire into his thoughts.

"I will sleep now," he said after a pause.

The minstrel rose to go, bowing a farewell.

"No," said Geoffroi; "stay there, make your bed in that faldestol to-night. I do not care to be alone. And, mark well! that if you hear any untoward noise, or should you hear a sound of men's voices praying, rouse me at once."

He turned his face towards the wall, and before long his deep breathing showed that sleep had come to him.

The candle began to burn very low and to flicker. The jongleur saw enormous purple shadows leap at each other across the room, and play, fantastic, about the bed. He rose and peered out of a narrow unglazed window in the thickness of the wall. The hot air from the room passed by his cheeks as it made its way outside. There was no lightning now, and the sky was beginning to be full of a colourless and clear light, which showed that dawn was about to begin. Far, far away in some distant steading, the jongleur heard the crowing of a cock.

As he watched, the daylight began to flow and flood out of the East, and close to the window he heard a thin, reedy chirp from a starling just half awake.

He turned round towards the room, thinking he heard a stir. He saw the elderly man on the bed risen up upon his elbow. His right hand pointed towards the opposite wall, at a space over the table. With a horrid fear thumping in his heart and sanding his throat, the minstrel saw that Geoffroi's eyes were open in an extremity of terror, and his nostrils were caught up and drawn like a man in a fit.

"My lord! my lord!" he quavered at him.

There was no sign that Geoffroi heard him, except for a quivering of his pointing, rigid finger. The minstrel took up a vessel of glass from the table, and flung it on the floor.

The crash roused the Baron. His arm dropped and his face relaxed, and, with a little groan, he fell face down in a swoon. The minstrel hopped about the room in an agony of indecision. Then he took the jug of wine, the only liquid he could find, and, turning the Baron on his back, he flung it in his face.

Geoffroi sat up with a sudden shout, all dripping crimson. He held out his red-stained hand. "What is this? What is this?" he cried in a high, unnatural voice. "This is blood on my hand!"

"No, my lord, it is wine," said the jongleur; "you fell into a deep swoon, and it was thus I roused you."

"Did you see him?" said Geoffroi. "Oh, did you see him by the wall? Christ shield us all! It was Pierce, a soldier of mine. His throat was cut and all bloody, and he made mouths like a man whose throat is slit in war."

"My lord, you are disordered," said the jongleur. "You ate pork at supper, a wonderful bad thing for the belly at night."

Geoffroi said never a word, but fell trembling upon his knees.

CHAPTER V

The three trees of Monkshood Glade.

How fresh the morning air was in the wood! A million yellow spears flashed through the thick leaves and stabbed the undergrowth with gold. A delicious smell of leaves and forest beasts scented the cool breezes, and birds of all colours sang hymns to the sun.

An early summer morning in a great wood! In all life there is nothing so mysteriously delightful. Where the leaves of the oaks and elms and beeches were so thick that they turned the spaces below into fragrant purple dusk, what soft bright-eyed creatures might lie hid! In the hot open glades brilliant little snakes lay shining, and green-bronze lizards, like toy dragons, slept in armour. The fat singing bees that shouldered their way through the bracken wore broad gold bands round their fur, and had thin vibrating wings of pearl. They were like jewels with voices.

Upon a piece of smooth grass sward, nibbled quite short by rabbits, which sloped down to a brook of brown and amber water, sat Lewin, the minter. His fine clear-cut face harmonised with all the beauty around, and he drank in the air as if it had been wine. There was a soft look in his eyes as of a man dreaming of lovely things. His face is worth a little scrutiny. The glorious masses of dark-red hair gave it an aureola, the long straight nose showed enormous force of character, but the curve of the lips was delicate and refined, and seemed to oppose a weakness. There was something dreamy, treacherous, and artistic in his countenance.

For an hour Lewin had come into the wood to forget his scheming and ambitions and to be happy in the sunlight. He plucked blades of grass idly and threw them into the brook. Once he looked up, feeling that something was watching him, and saw mild eyes regarding him from a thicket. It was a young fawn which had come to drink in the brook, and saw him with gentle surprise. He gave a hunting halloa, and immediately the wood all round was alive with noise and flying forms. Part of a herd of deer had been closing round his resting-place, and were leaping away in wild terror at his shout.

The forest became silent again, until he heard feet crackling on the leaves and twigs, and looking up saw a radiant vision approaching him. A tall, dark girl, lithe as a willow, was coming through the wood.

Lewin sprang up from the little lawn and went down the path to meet her, holding out his hands.

"Ah, Gundruda!" he said, "I have waited your coming. How fair you are this beautiful morning!"

"Go away," she said, with a flash of pearls. "That is what you say to every girl."

"Of course, Gundruda mine. I love all women; my heart is as large as an abbey."

"Then your fine speeches lose all their value, minter. But I have a message."

He dropped his banter at once. "Yes! yes!" he said eagerly.

"My lord goeth after a boar this afternoon with Sir Fulke, and my Lady Alice will be by the well in the orchard when they have gone."

"Good," said he, "there will I be also. Are Richard and Brian going hunting?"

"No; they will be hard at work with all the theows and men-at-arms fortifying the castle. Oh, Lewin, there is such a to-do! Last night as ever was, came a messenger to say Roger Bigot is coming to Hilgay to kill us all, and Christ help us! that is what I say."

A shrill note of alarm had come into her voice, for she had seen war before, and knew something of the unbridled cruelty that walked with conquerors. At that he put his arm round her waist and drew her close to him. They were a fine pair as they stood side by

The Serf

side in the wood. Lewin captured one pretty hand in his—a little, white, firm hand that curled up comfortably in his clasp. Then he kissed her on her soft cheeks.

"How beautiful you are," he said in a soft, dreamy voice, deep and rich. He strained her to him. "Oh, how strange and beautiful you are, Gundruda. I would that for ever you were in my arms. There is nothing like you in the world, Gundruda. You are worth kingdoms. Oh, you beautiful girl!"

She abandoned herself to his caresses, with closed eyes and quick shuddering breaths of pleasure. Suddenly the mellow notes of a horn in all their proud sweetness came floating through the wood, and this amorous business came to a sudden end.

Geoffroi was starting out to the hunt.

The two people in the wood went back to the castle by devious ways. They found that Lord Geoffroi with a few attendants had already left the castle and entered the forest.

The castle-works were humming with activity. The weapon smiths were forging and fitting arrow heads, and making quarels and bolts. The carpenters were building hoards, or wooden pent houses, which should be run out on the top of the curtains. The crenelets, which grinned between the roof and the machicolade at the top of Outfangthef, were cleared of all obstructions. A trèbuchet for slinging stones—invented in Flanders, and very effective at short range—was being fitted together on the roof of the Barbican. Hammers were tapping, metal rang on metal, the saws groaned, and a great din of preparation pervaded everything.

In one corner of the bailey a man was cutting lead into strips so that it could be more easily made molten and poured upon besiegers. In another a group were hoisting pitch barrels on to the walls with a pulley and tackle.

In and out of the great gateway rough carts were rattling every moment, full of apples and wheat from the farmhouses round.

A row of patient oxen were stabled in a pen, hastily knocked up with beams of fir, in one corner of the bailey. In the field by the castle side, the swine shrieked horribly as a serf killed them relentlessly, and in the kitchens the women boiled, dried, and salted before glowing wood fires.

Long before dawn, scouts on swift horses had been posting along the Norwich road, and messages had been sent to all the villeins proper to fulfil their pledge of service.

Tongues wagged unceasing.

"Come ye here, cripples, and give a hand to this beam."

"Have you gotten your money safe, minter? The bastard son a letcheth after coined monies."

"Aye, and after more things than coined monies. Gundruda, beauty, Roger hath a fat Turkman privy to him, and going always in his train. He will marry you to the black man!"

"By the rood, then, I'd as soon wed him as you!"

"Roger taketh with him always a crucet hûs, my son."

"And what is that, then, Father Anselm?"

"Know you not the crucet hûs? fight lustily, then, or you may know him too well. The crucet hûs, that is a chest which is short and narrow and shallow. Roger putteth men therein, and putteth sharp stones upon him so that all his limbs be brake thereby. My Lord Bigot loveth it. Also he useth the 'Lǎð and grim.' 'Tis a neck bond, my lad, of which two or three men had enough to bear one! It is so made that it is fastened to a beam. And Roger putteth a sharp iron round about the man's throat and his neck, so that he cannot in any direction sit or lie or sleep, but must bear all that iron."

"God's teeth! Father! you have a merry way of comfort."

"Truth is stern, Huber; fight then lustily, and get you shriven to-morrow."

"That will I, Father."

"And you, John and Denys, and Robert, all you soldiers. Come you to me ere this fight, and pay Holy Church her due fee, and have safety for your souls. An if you die then you will be saved men, and among the merry angels and my Lords the Saints, as good as they in heaven. An you go not to battle with hearts purged of sin, the divell will have every mother's son of you. Alas, how miserable and rueful a time will be then! And you who are whilom in shining armour-mail, with wine to drink, and girls to court for your pleasure, will lie in a portion of fire but seven foot long."

Thus, Anselm, the hedge priest, passing from group to group in beery exhortation.

Who knows how it affected them?

The heavenly sun still looks into the lowest valleys. The unclean hands of that false priest, unfaithful minister that he was, may have given the mass to a sick soul with great spiritual comfort. The bestial old man may have absolved dark men, penitent of their sins, because they themselves earnestly believed in his power.

As he sat in the chapel during that day, the mysterious powers conferred on him from Saint Peter himself, in unbroken succession, may, indeed, have flowed through him, giving grace.

Lewin lounged about the courtyard listening to his exhortations with amusement, yet not without wonder at the strange psychic force which moved the minds of these rough men. The crafty, sensual sentimentalist, of course, had no illusions about the abstract, yet the idea always fascinated him when it came. It was very grand and sonorous, he thought, this bondage to mystery, this ritual of the unseen. So lonely a man was he, immured in the impregnable fortress of his own brain, for there was no mental equal for him at Hilgay, that for mere mind-food he gave himself over to wild fancies. Our Lord upon the cross was more beautiful to him than to many devout believers, and he would have told you that he could hear the going of God in the wind. Sometimes he half-wondered if it were not true that Christ died.

He went into his mint, deserted now, and sat him down upon a bench in his little room. The sunshine cut its living way through the dust of the silent empty place. A whip lay upon the floor, where it had been thrown by an overseer of the theows who worked in the mint. There were flies upon it. He kicked the thing aside with disgust; it was a reminder of the stern terrible age in which he lived, and in which he felt so out of place. Depression began to flow over him in silent waves, until he remembered that he was to meet Lady Alice in the afternoon. That turned the current of his idle, discontented thoughts towards a more palpable thing. His secret wooing of the Norman lady who was so proud and stately was very dear to him, and the romance of it pleased him even more than the mere material joys he hoped some day to gain from it. Proud as she was, womanlike she at least deigned to listen to him, and his crafty brain schemed darkly to take opportunity as it came, and make her his own by treachery. He went out again among the busy workmen, and began to direct some smiths who were rivetting a suit of brass armour, engraved with a curious pattern of beetles and snakes in arabesque, which required delicate handling.

The weapon smiths were grumbling because they were short of hands for the heavier parts of their labour. Five or six of the most reliable serfs could not be found anywhere. Some one had seen them going into the forest, and it was supposed that they were acting as beaters for Geoffroi. Every one grumbled at the Baron. It was thought that this was no time for amusements. A boar would keep, herons would last till the world's end, deer would get them young every year till the world stopped. Every hour Roger Bigot came slowly nearer, and the men of Hilgay wanted the comfort of a master mind to direct and reassure them at a time like this.

The two squires fussed and raved, and stormed till the sweat stood in great drops upon them, but they could not get half the work out of the men that Geoffroi, or even Fulke, were able to. They had no personality and were ineffective, lacking that most potent and most powerful of human things. But every one did his best, nevertheless, and by "noon-meat" work had distinctly advanced, and already the castle began to wear something of an aspect of war.

It is extraordinary how a building or a place can be transformed in our minds by a few outward touches, combined with an attitude of expectation. If one has waited for a wedding in an almost empty church, the coming ceremony has an actual power of destroying the somewhat funereal aspect of the place. A single vase of flowers upon the altar seems swollen to a whole tree of bloom, the footsteps of a melancholy old man unlocking the rusty door, or spreading the priest's robes for him, is magnified into the beating of many feet. A crowd is created, expectant of a bride.

In a country lane on a hot summer afternoon, on Sunday, we say that a "Sabbath peace" is over all the land. The wind in the trees seems whispering litanies, and the soft voices of the wood-pigeons sound like psalms, the woods are at orisons, and the fields at prayer. As evening comes gently on, the feeling becomes intensified, though there is nothing but the chance lin-lan-lone of a distant bell to help it. The evening is not really more peaceful and gracious on the day of rest. The rooks wing home with mellow voices indeed, and the plover calls sweetly down the wind for his mate, but these are ordinary sounds. You may hear them on week days. The peace is in our own hearts, subjective and holy, informed by our own thoughts.

In the very air of the castle there was a tremulous expectation of war. Lady Alice, in her chamber, far away from the tumult, knew it. Little Gertrude, in the orchard, felt in her blood that the day was not ordinary; the very dogs sought wistfully to understand the excitement that pervaded everything.

At noon-meat, the jongleur, who had remained in the castle, blear-eyed and silent, got very drunk indeed. A madness of excitement got hold of him, and he sang war songs in a strident unnatural voice. The stern choruses rang out in the sunshine, with a pitiful whining of the crowth. All the afternoon the men hummed fierce catches as they went about their work. The day was cloudless and very hot. About five o'clock, when the sun's rays began to strike the ground slantingly, and the world was full of the curious relative sadness that comes with evening, the toilers knocked off for a rest. The pantler brought out horns of Welsh ale, and they sat round the well discussing the great impending event, the strength of the defences, the number of the enemy, the chances of the fight. The jongleur was lying insensible by the well-side, and a merry fool was bedabbling his shameless old face with pitch from a bucket, when the attention of every one in the castle was suddenly arrested by the distant but quite unmistakable sound of a horn.

A deep silence fell upon them all. Then they heard it again, no hunting mot or tuneful call of peace, but a long, keen, threatening note of alarm!

The thundering of a horse's feet growing ever nearer and nearer throbbed in the air. The sound seemed a great way off. Some one shouted some quick orders. The pins were pulled from the portcullis chains, so that upon releasing a handle it would fall at once. That was all they could do for the moment. They heard that the horseman was coming on at a most furious gallop. The sound came from the great main drive of the forest. Quick conjectures flew about among them all.

"Godis head! surely Roger is ten days away."

"So the scouts have said. He moveth very slowly. Oswald saw it with his own eyën."

The Serf

"We shall know before one should tell to twenty, listen!"

The news-bringer, whoever he might be, was now close at hand, and with startling effect he sent before him another keen vibratory note of his invisible horn. It seemed to come right up to the very castle gate, and to break in metallic sound at the feet of those standing near.

In a moment more they saw him turn out from among the interlacing forest trees, and come furiously down the turf towards them.

"It's Kenulf, the forester," shouted two or three voices at once. "Surely some one rides after him."

The rider was now close upon them, and vainly trying to pull in his horse. The animal was maddened by the goring of his spurs—long single spikes in the fashion of that time—and would not stop. So, with a shrill shout of warning and an incredible echoing and thunder of noise, he galloped over the drawbridge, under the vaulted archway of the gate tower, and only pulled up when he was in the bailey itself, and confronted with the great rock of the keep.

For a moment he could not speak in his exhaustion, but by his white face and haunted eyes they saw that he had some terrible news.

There was a horn of beer propped up against the draw-well, which some one had set down at the distant noises of the forester's coming. Brian de Burgh picked it up and gave it to the gasping fellow. Then he stammered out his news, striking them cold with amazement.

"My Lord Geoffroi is dead, gentlemen," said he. "He has been murdered. I came upon him standing by the three trees in Monkshood. He had an arrow right through his mouth, nailed to a tree was he, and the grass all sprent with him. Gentlemen, I came into the glade half-an-hour after I had seen my lord well and alive. He rode fiercely ahead of us after the boar, towards Monkshood. My lord loves to ride alone, and Sir Fulke followed but slowly, and set a peregryn at a heron on the way. But I pressed on faster, so that an Lord Geoffroi killed the boar, and when he had made the first cuts, I should do the rest. God help us all, and Our Lady too! I did come into the glade half a mile away from where the three trees stand. My eyën go far and they are very keen. There was a man, I could see, standing still, but as I blew a call he went swiftly into the underwood. Then came I to the trees and saw my lord standing dead. Sir Fulke and the train came up soon after, and they are bringing It home. Make you ready. Cwaeth he to me, that you were to make proper mourning, to light the torches and say the Mass, and have many lights upon the holy table. And so my lord shall the quicker find rest. Haste! haste! for soon they will be near, and there is scant of time withouten great haste. Take me to my lady, for I would tell her."

"No," said a girl, who was standing by, very hastily, "I will prepare her first," and with that Gundruda, with a face full of wonder, slipped away to the postern which led to the orchard.

So this was how the first tidings of Hyla's vengeance came to the castle.

Now the killing of Geoffroi de la Bourne happened in this way.

As one might imagine, there was no sleep for the serfs on the night before the attempt. From the time when they had stolen up the hill after the murder of Pierce to the coming of dawn was but short. They spent it round the dead fire among the noises of the night.

A great exultation was born in the heart of each man. Hyla showed them his blood-stained hands, with vulgar merriment at the sight, rejoicing in the deed. They were all animated with the lust of slaughter. Wild hopes began to slide in and out of their minds.

One could hardly expect anything fine—in externals—from these rough boorish men. Although their purpose was noble, and the feelings that animated them had much that owed its existence to a love for their fellows, a protest of essential human nature against oppression and foul wrongs, yet their talk was coarse and brutal about it all. This must be chronicled in order to present a proper explanation of them, but if it is understood it will be forgiven. No doubt the canons of romance would call for another kind of picture. The men would keep vigil, full of lofty thoughts, high words, and prayers to God. They would have spoken of themselves as Christ's ministers of wrath; the romancer would have prettily compared them to King David with his Heaven-ordered mission of vengeance. And yet King David, for example, mutilated the Philistines in a fearfully brutal way—it is for any one to read—and how much more would not these poor fellows be likely to shock and offend our nice sensibilities. No doubt it was horrible of Hyla to call up a sleeping puppy and make it lick Pierce's blood from his hands, but this story is written to make Hyla explicit, and Hyla was not refined.

Early in the morning the conspirators took a meal together before setting out to play their various parts in this tragedy. Harl was already far away with the women. Gurth was to go down to the river and take the swiftest punt away from the landing-place and hide in the reeds upon the other side. A whistle would summon him when Hyla and Cerdic came down to the water ready for flight. Gurth was to sink the other punts, to make pursuit impossible for a time.

Cerdic, Richard, and a third man called Aescwig were to lie in the wood to turn the boar, as well as they were able, towards the glade of Monkshood. They were lean, wiry men, swift of foot, and knew that they could do this. Cerdic had a swift dog concealed, for it was unlawed, which he used for poaching. It would help them. Hyla himself would lurk in the glade with his knife, waiting in the hope of his enemy.

After the first meal they slunk off to their posts with little outward emotion and but few words of parting. The clear cold light of the morning chilled them, and robbed the occasion of much of its excitement. But for all that went they doggedly towards their work.

For a certain distance Hyla went in company with the three beaters, but at a point they stopped, and he proceeded onwards alone.

When he had got far on upon his way to Monkshood he lay down deep in the fern to rest, and watched the sky between the delicate lace of the leaves.

He saw a tiny wine-coloured spider swinging from branch to branch like a drop of blood on a silver cord, the sunlight so irradiated it. The wild bees were already hard at work filling their bags of ebony and gold with the sweet juices of flowers. The honeysuckle swung its trumpets round the brown pillar of an oak, like censers of amber and ivory, shedding delicate incense on the air. The breezes carried the rich scents to and fro from tree to tree. Hyla felt weary now that the hour was so close at hand. He was not excited, nor did he even feel the slightest tremor of fear. He was simply indifferent and tired. He wanted to sleep for ever in this silent, sunlit place.

He was wearing Pierce's dagger round his waist, and he took it out to see if it was sharp enough. The stains of blood still held to it in films of brown and purple, but its point was needle-like, and the edge bitter keen. He put it down by his side upon a great fern tuft over which countless ants were hurrying. It fell among the ants as a streak of lightning falls among a crowd of men. Then, like some uncouth spirit of the wood, some faun, one might have fancied, he fell into a long, dreamless sleep.

He was awakened suddenly, when the sun was already at its height, by the sweet fanfaronade of distant horns. He glided away towards Monkshood swiftly and silently, a

The Serf

brown thing stealing through the undergrowth upon his malign errand. At last he came to the place he sought.

Monkshood Glade was a long narrow drive, carpeted with fine turf and surrounded with a thick wall of trees. In shape it was like the aisle of a cathedral. At the far end of the place it opened out into a half circle, like a lady chapel, and, to carry out the simile, where the altar should have been three great trees were standing in a triangle. The trunks of the trees grew within a hand's breadth of each other and formed a deep recess, with no entry save the one at the base of the triangle. Inside this place it was quite dark and cool.

Hyla crept into the undergrowth at the side of the glade, about twenty yards from the entrance to this little tree-cave, and lay waiting, crouching on his belly.

For an hour or two—it seemed ages to him—nothing happened whatever. The business of the wood went on all round, but there was no sound of human life. The waiting made him restive and uneasy. He began to remember how many the chances were that Geoffroi would not come that way. He began to see on how slender a possibility his hopes rested, and to wonder at himself and his companions for having trusted so great an issue to such a chance.

Then, quite suddenly, his heart leapt up and began to beat furiously, till the sound of its throbbing seemed to be surely filling all the wood. Peering out of the scrub he saw far down the glade a grey speck moving rapidly in his direction. It grew larger every moment as he watched, and next he saw that it was followed by a second and larger object, which almost immediately resolved itself into a man on horseback riding hard. In two minutes the boar and its pursuer were close upon him. He saw the boar galloping, with blood and foam round its tusks, and heard its harsh grunting. He could see its eyes as bright as live coals. Geoffroi was thundering twenty yards behind. Suddenly he saw the Baron taking aim at his quarry with a short, thick bow. He guided his horse, still in full career, a little to one side, by the pressure of his knees. It was a wonderful piece of horsemanship. He saw a quick movement of Geoffroi's arm, and, though the arrow sped too quickly for him to trace its course, the great boar with a hoarse squeal stumbled upon its fore-legs. It rose, staggered round in a circle, for the great forest beasts die hard, and then with a final squeal rolled over upon its side, with its hoofs stark and stiff in the air.

This took place between Hyla and the trees.

Geoffroi reined in his horse and, throwing his bow upon the ground, dismounted and ran towards the boar. He drew his hunting knife as he went.

As silently as a snake Hyla crept out of the undergrowth. Geoffroi's back was towards him and he was leaning over the boar with his knife. Hyla picked up the bow. The horse, heaving from its exertions, regarded him with mild eyes devoid of curiosity. Hyla took a barbed hunting shaft from the little quiver at the saddle side. He fitted it carefully to the bow. Suddenly the Baron stood up and was about to turn round when Hyla drew the bow-string to his shoulder, English fashion, and shot the arrow. It struck Geoffroi in the muscles of the left shoulder and went deep into him.

With a horrid yell of agony he spun round towards his unseen foe. Hyla had rapidly fitted another arrow to the bow and stood confronting him. For a moment the two men stood regarding each other. Then very slowly Geoffroi began to retreat backwards towards the trees. Hyla kept the arrow pointed at his heart.

"That was for Elgifu," he said.

Geoffroi reached the three trees, and went backwards into the recess. His eye rolled round desperately. Then he made a last effort. "Put that down," he roared with terrible authority. But the time had gone by when he could make Hyla cower.

"This is for Frija," said Hyla, and an arrow quivered in Geoffroi's mouth and passed through his head, transfixing him to the tree trunk behind.

A sudden impulse flooded the Serf's brain, quick, vivid, and uplifting: the tears started into his eyes though he knew not why.

Once more the bow-string twanged as a third arrow sank silently into the corpse. "For Freedom!" he whispered fearfully, wondering at himself.

Hyla stood watching the frightful sight with calm contemplation. The Baron dead and bloody was nothing. He began to feel a positive contempt for the man he had feared so long.

As he stood with a smile distorting his face, a horn rang out down the glade, and he saw that a horseman was riding hard towards him. Making the sign of the cross, he slipped into cover and began to fly swiftly through the wood.

CHAPTER VI

Per varios casus, per tot discrimena rerum, tendimus in LATIUM sedes ubi fata quietas ostendunt.

There is always and forever a haven we can win. In all the chances and turmoils of this life, howeversomuch we are tossed upon the seas of circumstance, somewhere, without doubt, there is peace.

For the intellect distracted and pierced through by every fresh morsel of knowledge, for the brain tired out by the senses, for the body full of the sickness, let us say, of a great town, somewhere the Fates have a quiet resting place. There is peace waiting. Let Alecto, Megaera and Tisiphone shriek and wail ever so loudly, they shall not break it.

Tendimus in Latium—we are all going towards Latium. For some of us it is the blessed peace of the grave, and others are to find it in this life. Somewhere there is peace!

Hyla felt an utter weariness of life and all its appeals as he fled through the forest. The hot wan wine of revenge that had been his blood was now cool and stagnant. That stern old devil-hearted man that he had made into a filthy corpse had passed away out of knowledge as if he had never been. The brain of the serf was all empty of sensation, save for that great weariness. His body was full of the mere instinct of self-preservation. The legs on which he ran, the arms which pushed aside the forest branches, the furtive eyes which sought for foes, all acted independently of his brain. Nature itself working in him bade him fly. For himself, had he thought about it, he would hardly have cared, even though he had been captured. But none the less was his fleeing swift and sure.

He twisted his tortuous way through the thick hazel shoots, which struck him in the face as he buffeted them, and his bare arms and legs were scarred and pricked in a thousand places with thorns from the trailing undergrowth.

When he had beat back to the other end of Monkshood, walking parallel to the glade, he heard voices close to him and the noise of a company of people entering the ride at the far end of the glade. By the three sinister trees, he heard the keen notes of a horn blowing in eager summons. Suddenly a new and terrible fear came to him. The dogs, which were whining all round, would most surely smell him in a moment. He could hear their excited movements on every side. He realised that he should have made a much greater detour, and that he had, in fact, stumbled into the very middle of his enemies.

He could see no way out of his perilous position, and felt that he was certain of immediate discovery. But the Fates, which were providing a short peace for him, willed that his capture was not yet to be. The urgent note of Kenulph's horn, half a mile away, attracted the dogs, and they gave tongue, and, dashing out of the cover, spread up the drive in a long line. Fulke, who was within ten yards of the hidden murderer, cheered them on.

"I can see figures," shouted a huntsman, "one, two horses. They must be my lord and Kenulph, and Sir Boar is dead. Come along, Sir Fulke, we are not very far behind after all!"

With that the whole company pressed out into the ride and thundered away, and Hyla was left solitary. The narrowness of the escape heartened him into fresh endeavour, and once more he began his swift career through the wood. After another mile of hard going, he sat for a moment. 'Twas then that he heard a low sibilant noise, like the hiss of a snake. He started up, looking round him on every side. He heard the sound again, and it seemed to come from the sky above.

He looked up into the depths of a beech tree above him, and presently there appeared a lean brown leg among the leaves. A body followed, and Cerdic dropped on to the turf.

"Well?" said Cerdic, "God be with you! What have you done?"

"Killed him," said Hyla with a curious pride, though he tried hard to appear unconscious of his great merit. "He's dead, sure enough. I well think he is in hell now—he and Pierce in the same fire."

"The Saints have watched thee with kind eyën that you did it, Hyla. In hell is my lord, and there a will lie, for Saint Peter that hath the key is not so scant of wit as to let him go. Let us thank Our Lady that did strengthen your arm."

"Yes, let us thank her," said Hyla. "I gave him two arrows, 'one for Elgifu,' I said, and 'this one for Frija,' I said. That was how I did it. So that he might be sure for what he died, you wist. Yes, that was just how I did it."

He had a curious shame which prevented a reference to the third shaft. He was not sure if Cerdic would have understood that arrow of Freedom. He hardly realised it himself.

"By Godis rood, you have done well, my friend. But pray, pray that you may be clean, and that Our Lady may wesshe you of blood guilt."

They knelt down, and became straightway enveloped in a mystery that was not of this world. The dead man in the tree-cave could not stir Hyla as this sudden invoking of God's mother, for he was certain that she was close by in the wood, listening.

Cerdic made prayer, because he was a man of quick wit and glib of tongue.

"O Lady of Heaven," said he, "we call upon you in our souls' need, and I will plainly tell you why. And that is this: Hyla has killed our Lord Geoffroi, for he did take his girls. And Lord Geoffroi has sorely oppressed us and beaten us, and so, dead is he. And we pray you that we be made clean of the killing in Godis sight. And if it may be so, we ask that you will say to the heavenly gateward that he should ne'er let our Lord Geoffroi therein. For Saint Peter knoweth not how bad a man he was. And we would that you wilt say by word that he be cast down with Judas and with all the devils into hell, Amen." And then in a quick aside to Hyla, "'Amen' fool, I did not hear you say it."

With that Hyla said "Amen" very lustily, and they both rose from their knees. "I am gride that I said no 'Amen,'" said Hyla, "but I was listening to the prayer. It was a wonderful good prayer, Cerdic."

"Yes," said the other, "I can pray more than a little when it so comes to me. Had I but some Latin to pray in I doubt nothing that I would get my own bocland back before I die. But come, we are far from safety yet. It gets late, we must go swiftly."

They met with no mishap, and saw no man till they were on the very outskirts of the wood, and not more than a couple of hundred yards from the stoke itself. They were about thirty yards from the main entrance to the wood, a road which was beaten hard with the coming and going of men and horses.

There they stopped for a consultation. Was it better, they asked each other, to gather some kindling wood and go boldly through the village as if upon the ordinary business of the day, or, on the other hand, to make a wide half circle, and reach the river a mile away from the landing-stage?

It was quite certain that as yet no news of the Baron's death had reached the castle. There could be no doubt of that. They might walk openly through the village with no suspicion. Yet, at the same time, they might very probably be met by a man-at-arms or one of the minor officials of the castle, and ordered to some work within its gates. It was a difficult question to decide upon hurriedly, and yet it must be settled soon. Every moment wasted in council meant—so they took it—a chance less for freedom. As they discussed the issue in an agony of indecision they both found that terror was flowing over them in waves. Cerdic's throat contracted and was pulled back again into a dry tightness. He cleared his throat at every sentence, as who should be about the nervous effort of a public speech.

As for Hyla, his stomach became as though it were full of water, and his bowels were full of an aching which was fearfully exciting and which at the same time, strangely enough, had an acute physical pleasure in it.

Their indecision was stopped by an event which left only one method of flight open to them.

As they tossed the chance back and forward to one another, debated upon it and weighed it, they heard the noise of a horseman passing by *ventre á terre*. As he passed he sounded his horn. They wormed their way to the road as they heard him coming, and saw that it was the forester Kenulph. His face was ashen grey and set rigid with excitement, and then both simultaneously saw that he was bearing the news to the castle.

He passed them like rain blown by the wind, and turning the corner was lost to their sight.

"This makes our way clear algates," said Cerdic. "Sith Kenulph rides to castle hall, we must be bold. It will take while a man might tell hundreds for them to take the news. He will hold all the castle in thrall. They will be forslackt for half-an-hour. He is there by now, all clad with loam and full of his news. Come out into the village and go down to river bank. We go to clear the brook mouth. It's all mucky and begins to kill the fish. Remember, that is what we go to do."

"I obey your heasts, Sir Cerdic," Hyla answered him with a smile. "Come, come upon the way. I think it matters not much one way or the other, but we may win our sanctuary by hardiment. Algates, we are ywrocken."

Revenged.

"Yes, that are we, and revenge is sweet. No more will he ill-use our girls, or burn us on the green. Surely he has a deep debt to pay."

While they had been speaking they had been gathering great armfuls of fallen twigs and branches, and soon they went slowly down the ride with these. The frowning gates of the castle came into their view, but Kenulph had already entered them, and the very guards had left the gates. They passed by to the right, and came on to the green. One or two women were busy washing linen at the doors of the houses, but save for them no one was about.

They passed the long walls of the castle, skirting the moat, by which a smooth path ran, till they came to the fields. There they were stopped for a few minutes. One Selred, a serf who tended swine, came out of the field where his charges dwelt. He was a half-witted creature, but little removed from the swine themselves. He carried a spear head, broken off a foot down the shaft, and this had been sharpened on a hone of hard wood for a weapon with which to kill the swine. He pointed to the row of dead animals which lay stark and unclean on one side of the field.

"Nearly fifty," said he, "have I killed this day for siege vittaille, to their very great dreriment. Holy Maid! never did you hear such squealing."

They shook him off after a time, but with difficulty. He was infinitely proud of his achievement. "I do love pig's flesh," he gibbered after them as they fled down the hill.

From the castle there now came the shrill notes of a tucket, and then the castle bell began to toll furiously, and a confused noise of shouting floated down the hill. When they hurried to the landing-stage they found that the boats had been duly scuttled. Here and there a gunwale projected out of the water, and on the stones lay the windac of a crossbow with which holes had been made in the boats.

Hyla gave a long, low whistle, and waited for Gurth to glide out of the reeds bordering the great fen. There was no reply, and the two fugitives looked at each other in alarm. Then Cerdic whistled rather louder, but still the welcome sight of the boat did not come to them.

"Something has happened to the mome," Cerdic said, "I am sure that he would not forslowe us like this if a were safe."

"What shall we do?" asked Hyla.

"I do not know," said Cerdic, his courage oozing out of him every moment. Their position was certainly sufficiently perilous. There was, as yet, nothing to connect them with the crime, but half-an-hour might alter everything. It was, moreover, quite certain that, in a search, one party at least would be sent down to the river.

They stood there gazing at each other in great alarm.

"I have a great fear that we are lost," Hyla said.

"Indeed, I believe so," answered the other, with strained, terrified eyes.

Both of them felt that they were hard in the very grip of unkind circumstance. They shook like river-side willows when the wind blows.

Now as they stood together communing as to what they should do, and with a great sinking of heart, it chanced that their faces were turned towards the river, away from the castle. They looked most eagerly towards the reeds upon the other side.

The river ran sluggishly like oil, and there was no breaking up of its surface. Here and there some dancing water-flies made a tiny ripple, but that was all.

Suddenly a great fish leapt out of the middle water high into the air. A flash of silver, a glimpse of white belly, and with a loud report it was gone. Sullen circles widened out and broadened towards them. Then they saw at the very place where the bream had disappeared the still surface of the water was violently agitated. They watched in amazement. A great black object heaved slowly up into view, full six feet long. It was the body of Pierce, the man-at-arms, all swollen by water. The face was puffed into an enormous grotesque, and the open eyes seemed cognisant of them.

The faces of the two serfs became ashen white, and they looked at each other in terrible fear.

"Christ, what a visnomie!" said Cerdic.

"God shows us that we are to die. My lord will be ywrocken" said Hyla.

"See how it seems alive."

"Yes, that does it. I can see the hole in's neck. The fishes have been at it."

"Oh, courage, courage! Our Lady never means us to die, whistle for Gurth once more. Perchance he is nearer now, perchance he is nearer, and, not knowing we are here, cometh not."

"I cannot sound a note, my breath is hot and my lips are very dry. Whistle you for me."

The Serf

Just then a noise of shouting behind their backs made them both wheel round swiftly. Half-way down the hill a group of men-at-arms were running towards them.

Cerdic gave a great wail of despair.

One of the soldiers dropped upon his knee, and a long arrow came past them singing like a great wasp. It ricochetted over the water into the reeds beyond. The soldiers were now a hundred and fifty yards away, shouting fiercely as they came on.

Hyla turned a last hopeless glance to the river. Just as he did so a long nose shot out of the reeds, and the punt they had waited for glided swiftly towards them.

"Hallo, hallo!" Cerdic yelled in an agony of excitement. "Quick, quick, else we die!"

There was a sudden jar as the prow of the punt collided with the masonry. The two serfs leapt into it. Gurth took the long pole and plunged it deep into the water. The muscles grew rigid on his bare back and stood out upon his arms as he bent for one mighty stroke. The soldiers were only twenty yards away. With an incredible slowness, so it seemed to the fugitives, the arms of the punter began to lengthen as the boat moved. In another second the propelling impulse gathered force and speed, and just as the first man arrived upon the landing-stage it glided rapidly over the water. There was a thud as it struck the floating body, and a horrid liquid bubbling, and then in another second they entered the passage and the reeds hid them from view. Gurth sank down, deadly sick, upon the floor of the punt, and the pole, held by one hand only, dragged among the rushes with a sound like a sickle in corn.

The three men crouched in the bottom of the boat, listening to the angry clamour on the opposite shore. An arrow or two passed over their heads, and one fell from a height into the very prow of the boat, but none of them were touched. There was not an ounce of courage among them. They had no strength to go on.

The castle bell away on the hill-top still rang loudly, and the shrill metallic notes of the tuckets called and answered to each other all round.

As they lay in the reeds not thirty yards from their pursuers, these noises of alarm filled them with fear. A voice rang out from the excited babble across the river and flung an echoing and malignant threat at them.

Although they could see nothing, the whole scene was painted for them with noise. They heard the voices sink into a quick murmur of conversation, and then hurried footsteps sped up the hill with messages for the castle.

Still they stayed trembling in the punt and made no effort to escape. All the weight of the terrible traditions that overhung their class was upon them. The great effort they had made, their incredible boldness, now left them with little more spirit, in spite of their good fortune, than whipped dogs. The moment was enough, for the moment they were safe from capture, and the voices of the soldiers—how terribly near!—did not stir them to action.

It was only when their peril became imminent that they were roused from their apathy. Sounds of activity floated over to them. A voice was giving directions, and then there was a shout of "Now," followed by a harsh, grating noise. The serfs realised that the soldiers had been able to drag one of the sunken punts on to the landing-stage. Almost immediately a noise of hammering was heard. They were repairing the boat.

At that shrill, ominous sound Cerdic rose from the bottom of the punt trembling with excitement. "Men," he said in a deep startled voice, "we have been here too long, and death is like to come our way. Oh, faint hearts that we have been, and the Saints with us so long, and the Holy Maid helping us! Come, silent now! take poles and let us get away. I know the fens better than those divells."

The Serf

So confident was his voice and so burning with excitement, that in one moment it lashed their cowardice away. Hyla sprung towards the stern pole and Gurth lifted the other, then, with hardly a movement save a few tiny splashes, the boat glided slowly away into the heart of the fen. The voices of the soldiers became fainter and more faint till they could hear them no more.

The ringing blows of the hammer pursued them a little further, until in a few minutes those also died away, and they were alone in the fen.

All round them the great reeds rose and whispered, enormous bulrushes with furry heads like young water-rats nodded towards them as they raced for their life down those dark mysterious water-ways. Deeper and deeper into the heart of the great fen sped the boat. Gurth and Hyla worked with the precision of machines. There was a wonderfully stimulating effect in the rhythm of the action. The water became a deep shining black, showing incalculable depths below. In order to propel the boat at all they had to skirt the very fringe of the morass, for there only could the poles find bottom. At each heave and lift, under which the punt kicked forward like some living thing, the poles came up clotted and smeared with stinking black mud, undisturbed before for hundreds of years. Sometimes, at a deeper push, the mud was a greyish white and studded with tiny shells, tokens which the great grey sea had left behind to tell that once it had dominion there.

All wild nature fled before their racing approach. A hundred yards ahead, even in those tortuous ways, fat unclean birds of the fen rose heavily and clanged away over the marshes. As the throb of the poles came near them, the fish shouldered each other in flight. Every now and again they rushed over a still, wicked pool teeming with fish, and the rush of their passage made white-bellied fish leap out of the water in terror. Once they saw a great black vole, as large as a rabbit, swimming in the middle of the water. He heard them coming, and turned a wet smooth head to look; then with a twinkle of his eyes he dived and disappeared.

Gradually the speed of the boat slackened as the two men grew tired. The excitement of the day began to tell on them, and they felt in their arms how weary they were. Cerdic, who perhaps by virtue of his years or personal magnetism seemed to be indubitably their leader, saw it in their faces. He saw that not only were they physically worn out, but that energy was going from their brains also.

"Stop you," said this shrewd person. "We are far from them now. It is time for rest and belly food." Nothing loth, they put down the punt poles, and pushed the nose of the boat into a little bay of reeds, out of the main water.

"Food?" said Hyla, "with all my heart, I did not know you had any. Where is it pight?"

Cerdic gave a little superior grin. He took up a skin wallet which lay by his side and produced the materials for a feast. Six great green eggs, stolen from a sitting duck which had belonged to the ill-fated Pierce, were the staple food. Boiled hard and eaten with black bread and some scraps of cold meat, they were a banquet to the fugitives. For drink they had nothing but marsh water, which they sucked up through a hollow reed. It was blackish and rather stagnant, but it refreshed them mightily.

"And how far have you got now, do you think?" said Gurth.

"Near half way," answered Cerdic, "but it has been easy going, and we shall not get such free water now. It is a back way to Icomb that we have come by up till now. Whybeare there was a broad passage, a great stretch of water, but that was in King William's time, when boats brought corn from Edmundsbury. Now the monks have corn-land of their own, and corn comes from Norwich also. The passage is all grown with weed and reeds, and no man may go up it in any vessel."

"Where must we go, then?" Hyla asked him.

"Nor'wards for some miles, taking any way we can that is open. Then we shall come to the lake of Wilfrith, and beyond that is the Abbey."

"What is Wilfrith lake, and who was he?" said Hyla. "I have been upon its water, but I do not know why it is called that. Also, it has a bad name, and they say spirits are seen upon it."

Cerdic crossed himself at that.

"Wilfrith was once Prior of Icomb," he said, "a good priest, and much loved by God. Upon a day he was walking by the lake side, when he was seized by lawless men and robbed of his gold cross, and left bound to a tree in the forest, near the monastery. It was evening, and he could see the robbers getting into their boats to cross the lake. So he prayed to God. 'Lord,' he cried, 'I have not loved Thee enough. Deliver me from my need, and with Thy help I will so correct and frame my life that henceforth I may serve Thee better.' As he prayed, and when the thieves were about half way over the lake, there came a great black hand up out of the water and seized the boat and dragged it into the depths. At the same time his bonds fell from him, and he became free."

"A black hand," said Hyla uneasily, "that would be a fearful thing to meet with."

"We shall not do so," said Cerdic, "for I believe that the Great Ones are helping us to-day. Who knows that they are not with us now? We have killed Lord Geoffroi for his cruelty and sins, for all he was a lord. Do you think Lord Christ would have let him be killed if he had not wished it? Not he. He's no fool. I tell you," he said, cracking the shell of his second egg, and with great sincerity in his voice, "I tell you that like as not Sir Gabriel or Lord Abdiel, or one of the angels is flying over the boat with his sword in's hand and his tucket on his shoulder."

They all looked up to see if the angel was there, but only a little wind rustled the tops of the rushes, though the sky above was beginning to be painted with evening.

They prattled there a little longer, willing that their rest should be complete.

Now, at eventide, all the fishes began to rise at the flies, and the waters became like stained-glass, and peace was over all that wild scene.

The voices of the serfs insensibly dropped, and made low murmurs, no louder than the sounds of the cockchafers and long-mailed water-flies that now boomed and danced over the fen.

The moon was slowly rising when they put out again on the last stage of their journey, punting with less haste, but making good going, nevertheless. They were in excellent spirits.

CHAPTER VII

"Introibo ad altare Dei."

"Surely," said a monk of Bec, "God has made the evening beautiful and full of lights, so that we may think on Him at that time, and as we watch the very gates of heaven in the sky, pray to our Father that we may some day be there also."

It was a holy and wonderful evening-time, as the boat glided on through the vast shining solitudes. The heavenly influence stole into the souls of the three serfs, and purged them of all fear and sorrow. Imagine the enormous change in their lives. A curtain seemed to have fallen over all that they had known. The noise of the horrible castle, the sharp orders, the lash of the whip, the fœtid terrors of the stoke, had all vanished as if they had never been. Before them might lie a wonderful life, possible happiness, freedom. At any rate, for the moment they were free, and the sky shone like the very pavements of heaven.

All three of them noticed the beautiful sunset with surprise, as if it were a thing that had never been before their eyes till now.

Day by day, as their work at Hilgay was drawing to a close, the sky had been as beautiful as this. The sky had been all gold and red, and copper green and great purple clouds had passed over it like a march of kings. But they had never seen it until now. Freedom had come to them and whispered in their ears. She had passed her hands over their eyes, and they began to know, with a sort of wonder, that the world was beautiful. Nor was this all of the gracious message. Everything was altered. Hyla, it will be remembered, had a face of little outward intelligence. He had, in fact, the face of a serf. But the latent possibilities of it had been made fine realities within the last few hours. What he had done, his own independent action, woke up the God in him, as it were. His voice was not so slipshod. Round his mouth were two fine lines of decision, his lips did not seem so full, his eyes were alert and conscious.

Gurth was a sunny-haired, nut-brown youth, straight as a willow wand, and of a careless, happy disposition. But he had been cowed by the stern and cruel subjection under which he had lived. One could see the change in him also. He flung his arms about as he punted, with the graceful movements of a free man who felt his limbs his own. Little smiles rippled round his lips, he looked like a young man thinking of a girl.

It is obviously most difficult for us to project ourselves with any certainty into the mood of these three men. The whole conditions of our lives are so absolutely different. But we can at any rate imagine for ourselves, with some kindness of spirit, how joyous these tremulous beginnings of freedom must have been! The modern talk of "freedom," the boasting of nations that enjoy it, does not mean very much to us. The thing is a part of our lives, we do not know how much it is. But who shall estimate the mysterious splendour that irradiated the hearts of those three poor outcasts?

The long supple poles went swishing into the water and the boat leapt forward. They rose trailing out of the water, and the drops fell from them in cascades of jewels, green, crimson, and pearl. Every now and again the turnings of the passage brought them to a stretch of water which went due west. Then they glided up a sheet of pure vivid crimson, and at the end the fiery half-globe of the sun.

Just as the sun was dipping away they rested again for half-an-hour, and when they went on it was dark. At last, when the night was all velvet black and full of mysterious voices, they turned a corner, and suddenly the punt poles could find no bottom, though they went on with the impetus of the last stroke.

A greater silence suddenly enveloped them, they saw no reeds round them, the horizon seemed indefinite.

"This is Wilfrith Lake," said Cerdic, "and we are near home."

Now an unforeseen difficulty presented itself. The lake was far too deep to punt in, and they had no oars. For the next hour their progress would be slow. Cerdic came to the rescue. With his knife he cut a foot of wood from each punt pole, with infinite labour; then he fashioned the tough wood into four stout pegs. Gurth drilled two holes in the gunwales of the punt, with the dagger which had been taken from Pierce. Then they hammered the pegs into the holes and made rough rowlocks. There were no seats in the punt, and the thin poles did not catch the water very well, but by standing with their faces towards the bow they were able to make slow but steady progress.

It was a little unnerving. They could not be sure of their direction except in a very general way. It was chilly on this great lake, and very lonely. Hyla, and Gurth also, began to think of the great black hand. Who knew what lay beneath those sombre waters?

Never before in their lives had they spent such an exciting day. Hardy as they were, inured to all the chances and changes of a rough day, they began to be rather afraid, and their nerves throbbed uncomfortably. Indeed, it is little to be wondered at. They were men and not machines of steel. Once a great moth, which had strayed far out over the waters, flapped into Hyla's face with an unpleasant warmness and beating of wings. He gave a little involuntary cry of alarm, which was echoed with a quick gasp from the other two.

"What is that?" said Cerdic.

"Only a buterfleoge," Hyla answered him. "For the moment I was fearful, but it was nothing, and as light as a leaf on a linden tree."

The other two crossed themselves without answering, and strained their eyes out into the dark.

"Hist!" said Gurth suddenly. "Listen! Cannot you hear anything? Wailing voices like spirits in pain!" They shipped the poles and bent out over the boat listening intently.

Something strange was occurring some half a mile away, judging from the sound. A long musical wail came over the water at regular intervals, and it was answered by the sound of many voices.

As they watched and listened in terror, they saw a tiny speck of light on a level with the water, which appeared to be moving towards them. The voices grew louder, and then with a gasp of relief the fugitives heard the tones of men singing.

"They are the fathers from Icomb," said Hyla; "they are looking for us, and have come out in their boats."

In the still night a deep voice chanted a verse of the sixty-ninth psalm. The sonorous words of comfort rolled towards them:

"*Deus in adjutiorum meum intende: Domine, ad adjuvandum me festina.*"

Then came the antiphon in a great volume of sound: "*Confundantur et revereantur: qui quaerunt animam meam.*"

The single voice complained out into the night: "*Avertantur retorsum, et erubescant; qui volunt mihi mala.*"

The many voices replied in thunderous appeal: "*Avertantur statim erubescentur: qui dicunt mihi, euge, euge!*"

Then the cantor sang with singular and penetrating sweetness: "*Exsultent et laetantur in te omnes qui quaerunt te: et dicant semper, magnificetur Dominus, qui diligunt salutare tuum.*"

And the poor monks answered him of their estate: "*Ego vero egenus et pauper sum. Deus adjuva me!*"

The boat of the fathers was now quite close to the serfs. The lantern in the bows sent out long wavering streaks of light into the dark, and the many voices were full, and clear, and strong.

"Ahoy! ahoy!" shouted Cerdic in tremulous salutation.

The singing stopped suddenly, save for the cantor, who quavered on for a word or two of the *Gloria*. "What are you?" came over the water.

"Hyla of Hilgay, with Cerdic and Gurth."

There was a full-voiced shout of welcome, and the great boat came alongside with a swirl of oars.

The lantern showed many dark figures, some of them wearing the tonsure, and rows of pale faces gazed at the three serfs with eager interest.

A tall man in the bows of the boat, with a thin, sharp face peered at them. "We expected you," he said simply, "and we prayed that you might come, Benedicite! What news bring you? What is done? Christ be with you! Have you struck the tyrant and avenged the blood of the saints whom he slew?"

"Father," said Hyla, "I did kill the divell, sure enough. With two arrows—'One for Frija,' I said, and 'this for Elgifu.' I have blood guilt upon me."

The man in the bows lifted his right hand and stretched out two fingers and a thumb. They saw he was a priest. Then he said the *Confiteor*:

"*Misereatur tui omnipotens Deus, et dimissis peccatis tuis, perducat te ad vitam aeternam.*"

And every man in the boat answered "Amen."

Then the priest changed his tone, and became brisk and business-like.

"You have lost your oars, fools," he said. "Or, perhaps, you brought none. Should'st have remembered the lake. Take a stern rope and we'll tow ye home like knights. Now then, brethren, ye have heard the news, God in His mercy hath sent power to these poor men and aided their arm, so that they have slain the burner of His priests and ravisher of poor maids. God has answered our prayers. Sing we to Him then a song of thanksgiving. Sing up every man-jack of you, for God has wonderfully dealt with these poor men."

And then with a sudden crash of sound they began to sing the greatest of all hymns, the *Te Deum*.

"*Te Deum Laudamus: te Dominum confitemur,*" pulsed and rang through the night in glad appeal. So fervent and joyous was the song, the monks sang it so merrily, and withal it was to such a good and jocund tune, that Hyla was overcome entirely. He knelt in the swiftly-moving punt sobbing like a little child. Once he raised his face to heaven, and behold, there was a bright white moon silvering all the sky!

Very soon they came to the opposite shore of the lake, indeed, before the final "*In te Domine.*"

The shore sloped gradually down to the lake's edge in a smooth sweep of grass sward which met the water without any break. A few yards up the slope high trees fringed a road which led to the Abbey on the hill-top. Icomb was, in fact, a low island about half a mile square. Its highest point was hardly out of the fen mists. Round about in the county, the place was always spoken of as an Abbey, though it was, as a matter of fact, no more than a Priory, and of no great importance at that.

Icomb was a new offshoot from Saint Bernard's famous Abbey of Clairvaux. Very little was as yet known of the Cistercians, and the monks of Icomb were regarded as mysterious and not altogether desirable people by the great religious houses at Ely and Medhampstede.

It was part of the Cistercian rule that the founders of an abbey should choose some lonely, dismal place for their home. The idea was not entirely that of the eremite, for the Cistercians were improvers as well as colonists.

Icomb was the most lonely place in all the Eastern counties that the monks could have chosen for their retreat from the perils and unrests of this world. The low, tree-crowned island hill, surrounded by vast waters, protected by savage swamps, hidden in the very heart of the fen, was ideal for their purpose.

In that time not even churches were safe from lawless bandits like Geoffroi de la Bourne or Roger Bigot. Although men like these were belted knights of noble family, and still kept up much of the ceremonial of their position, they were little more than robbers, and instances abound of their sacrilege.

But as yet none of them had troubled Icomb. The place was very inaccessible; it was excellently protected by Nature, the defences were very strong, and the garrison a fine one.

The lay-brothers or *fratres conversi* were lusty and used to arms. Many of them had borne a pike in battle before entering into the peace of the Church. Then there were a goodly number of serfs and fenmen employed on the daily business of the Priory, who would all fight to the death if it were attacked.

No better sanctuary could be found for fugitives. Richard Espec, the prior of Icomb, was always ready to extend the hand of welcome to the oppressed. The time was so black and evil, such a horrible cloud of violence hung over England, that he felt it his bounden duty to make his house a refuge.

The Priory, like all Cistercian monasteries, was surrounded by a strong wall for defence. The buildings, though large and well built, were of a studied plainness. No glorious tower rose into the sky, but little ornament relieved the bareness of the walls. By the rules of that order only one tower, a centralone, was permitted, and that, so it was ordained, must be very low. All unnecessary pinnacles and turrets were absolutely prohibited. In the chapel the triforium was omitted, and the windows were of plain glass with no colour. The crosses on the altars were of simple wood, and the candlesticks of beaten iron. Lewin would have been absolutely disgusted with Icomb.

The buildings consisted of the chapel, a chapter-house adjoining, connected with the church by a sacristy and a cell, the refectory and monks' dormitories, and the calefactorium, or day-room. Here the monks met in the day-time to gossip and to grease their sandals. In winter it was warmed by flues set in the pavement. The centre of the block of buildings was occupied by the cloisters and a grass plot.

The two boats were hauled up the slope, and the party went singing up the hill in the moonlight. The dark trees which lined the road nodded and whispered at their passing, as the holy song went rolling away among the leaves. The three serfs felt wonderfully safe and happy. The dark depths of the thicket had no suggestion of a lurking enemy, the moon shone full and white over the road, and above, the tall buildings of the Priory waited for them. The hand of God seemed leading them, and His presence was very near.

They came to the gateway and the priest beat upon it with his walking-stick. In a moment it swung open, and they heard the porter say "Deo gratias," thanking Heaven that it had afforded him the chance of giving hospitality. Then, according to use, he fell upon his knees with a loud "Benedicite."

The priest who had met them went at once in search of the prior. In a minute or two he returned, saying that the prior was praying in the chapel, but that he would see them in the sacristy when he rose.

They were shown into a low, vaulted room with oak chests all round, and lit by a horn lantern. A half-drawn curtain separated it from the church, and through a vista of pillars they could see the high altar gleaming with lights, and a bowed figure on the steps before it. The rest of the great place was in deep shadow.

They sat down upon one of the chests and waited. A profound silence enveloped them, the wonderful and holy silence of a great church at night. A faint, sweet smell of spices pervaded the gloom.

Suddenly they realised that they were tired to death. All three leant back against the wall in motionless fatigue and let the silence steal into their very blood. They ceased to think or conjecture, and let all their souls be filled with that great, fragrant peace.

At last they heard some one coughing in the church, waking shrill echoes, and in a moment the sound of approaching footsteps. Richard Espec came in at the door. He was a short, enormously fat man, with a shrewd, benevolent face. He wore a white scapular and a hooded cowl, and on his breast gleamed the gold cross of Wilfrith. He blessed them as he entered, and they fell on their knees before him. He turned and drew the curtain over the door, shutting out the view of the church, and then sitting down upon a chest, regarded them with a penetrating though kindly glance.

"Ye are tired, my men," he said. "I can see it in your faces. Sit down again. Now I know from Harl, your friend, and Gruach, the wife of Hyla, what business you went out to do. Which of you is Hyla?"

"I am Hyla, father."

"Well?"

"Father," said poor Hyla, trembling exceedingly, "I have killed Lord Geoffroi."

The prior gave a slight start, and said nothing for a minute or two. At last he spoke.

"I may be wrong, Hyla, but I wist not. I do tell you here that I believe our Heavenly Father has guided your arm, and that you were appointed an instrument of His hand. Therefore, to-morrow you shall confess to one of the brethren and receive absolution for your act, if indeed you need it. And you shall be with your friends, servants to the monastery, well treated. Outside the walls live many of our fishermen and farm hands, and you and your wife and daughters shall be given a hut there. And I charge you three that you live well and wisely with us. Remember, ye come from Satan his camp, and from among evil men, and that we were not as they. But I well think you will be good and live for Christ. Not in fear of God's anger, but in pleasure and joy at His love and kindly *régime*, so that at last ye may join the faithful who have scand to heaven before you. I will pray for you, my sons, very often. Now I will call Brother Eoppa, our hospitaller, and he will give you food and a nipperkin of wine. But before you go to your rest I ask you to pray with me."

He knelt down, panting a little with the exertion, and said the Lord's Prayer in Latin. Then he opened a door which led into the cloisters. Outside the door the light of the sacristy lantern showed a thin sheet of copper hanging from an iron bracket. The prior struck this with his clenched fist, and a brother came running in answer. He committed the serfs to him with a kind smile, and then went back into the great, silent church.

The four went down the North Walk together, and turned into the western cloister. A door leading out of this led them into the hospitium, where the lay-brother, who had charge of guests, presently joined them.

"Hungry?" said he, "I think well you must be that. Brother Maurice is broiling fish for ye, and that is a dish that Saint Peter himself loved. It would be waiting now, but that kitchen fire was very low. Here is wine, a nipperkin for each of you."

Presently they heard footsteps echoing in the cloister.

"I can smell your fish in the slype," said the hospitaller. "It's here. Fall to, and bless God who gives ye a fat meal."

He left them alone to eat, meeting another lay-brother in the cloister and going with him into the kitchen.

"Dull fellows, I call them," said he.

"Yes. They do not look very sensefull."

"Poor men, they have been evilly used, no doubt. They have rid the world of as bloody a devil as ever cumbered it. I mind well what he did to the hedge priest in Hilgay fen," and they fell talking of Geoffroi and his iniquities with bated breath.

Hyla, Cerdic, and Gurth made a great meal.

"It's wonderful well cooked," said Gurth.

"And good corn-bread," said Cerdic.

"Never did I drink such wine before," said Hyla, and without further words, they fell asleep upon three straw mattresses placed for them against the wall. The tolling of the

The Serf

bell in the centralone, calling the monks to the night-offices, did not disturb them. Nor were they assailed by any dreams. "Nature's dear nurse," tended them well at the close of that eventful night.

CHAPTER VIII

"And after that, the Abbot with his couent
Han sped hem for to burien him ful faste."

They buried Geoffroi de la Bourne, the day after his murder, in a pit dug in the castle chapel, under the flags. The bell tolled, the tapers burnt, the pillars of the place were bound round with black. Upon the altar was a purple cloth. Dom Anselm got him a new black cope for the occasion, and was sober as may be. After the coffin had been lowered, and the holy water sprinkled upon it, all the company knelt at a Mass said for the repose of that dark soul.

"Do Thou, we beseech Thee, O Lord, deliver the soul of Thy servant from every bond of guilt." Anselm went down to the grave-side from the altar-steps, while page-boys, acolytes for the time, carried the cross and the holy water.

It was not a very impressive ceremony. I do not think that the little chapel made it appear sordid and tawdry. It was not the lack of furniture for ritual. Some more subtle force was at work. God would not be present at that funeral, one might almost say.

After the service was over and the Mass was said, Fulke summoned Lewin and Anselm to him in his own chamber. The squires were not there, for the preparations for the siege were being pushed on rapidly, and they were directing them.

The three men sat round a small, massive table drinking beer. "Well," said Fulke, "it is most certain that it was this theow Hyla. Everything points to that. As far as we have found, he was the chief instrument in the plot. For, look you, it was to him, so that boy said before he died, that the others looked. He seemed to be the leader. By grace of Heaven all the rogues shall die a very speedy death, but for him I will have especial care."

"The thing is to catch him," said Dom Anselm, "and I wist no easy job. Are you going to pull down Icomb Priory?"

"I would do that, and burn every monk to cinders if I had time and men enough."

"That is impossible," said Lewin. "I have been there to buy missals for barter from their scriptors. My lord, it's in the middle of a lake, up a steep hill, and with a great moat and twin outer walls. We could never come by Icomb."

"Also," said Anselm, "we have but a week at the most before we are within these four walls with no outgoing for many a day. The Bastard will be here in a week."

"What's to do?" Fulke asked gloomily.

Lewin contemplatively drained a fresh rummer of beer. "This is all I can think of," said he. "These serfs have fled to Icomb, and, no doubt, have been taken in very gladly by the monks. We are not loved in these parts, Lord Fulke. But Richard Espec is not going to keep them in great ease with wine and heydegwyes. They will work for their bread. Outside the monastery walls there is a village for the servants, on the edge of the corn-lands. Now see, lord. A man may go begging to Icomb, may he not? For the night he will sleep in the hospitium. After that, if he wanteth work, and will sign and deliver seisin to be a man of Icomb for three years, I doubt nothing but the monks will have him gladly. They do ever on that plan. He will live in the village. Well, then, that night let there be a swift boat moored to the island, and let the first man come to it and tell those therein where this devil Hyla lies. The rest is very easy. A man can be bound up and thrown into the boat in half-an-hour, and then we will have him here."

"Ventail and Visor!" said Fulke, "that is good, Lewin, we will have him safe as a rat. But I have another thought too. I had forgotten. The man's daughter Elgifu is still in the castle. It is not fitting that she should live."

"'Tis but a girl," said Lewin, the sentimentalist.

Fulke snarled at him. "Girl or no girl, she shall die, and die heavily. By the rood! I will avenge my father's murder so that men may talk of it."

His narrow face was lit up with spite, and he brought his hand down upon the table with a great blow.

"Perhaps you are right, my lord," said Lewin; "it is as well that she should be killed. I only thought that she is a very pretty girl."

"There are plenty more, minter."

He went to the door and opened it, shouting down the stairs. A man-at-arms came clattering up to him, making a great noise in the narrow stone stairway. He ordered that the girl should be brought to him, and presently she stood in front of them white and trembling, for she saw their purpose in their eyes.

"You are going to be hanged, girl," said Fulke, "and first you shall be well whipped in the castle yard. What of that? Do you like that? Hey?"

She burst into pitiful pleadings and tremulous appeals. Her voice rang in agony through the room. "I cannot die, lord," she said. "Oh, lord, kill me not. My lord, my lord! my dear lord! For love of the Saints! I cannot bear it!"

The brute watched her with a sneer, and then turned to the man-at-arms. "Tie her up to the draw-well, strip her naked, and give her fifty stripes. Then hang her, naked, on the tree outside the castle gate."

The man lifted her up in his arms, a light burden, and bore her shrieking and struggling away.

Fulke leant back against the wall with a satisfied smile. Dom Anselm had composed his features to an expression of stern justice, Lewin was white and sick. Human life went for very little in those days, but he did not like this torture of girls.

Gundruda, the pretty waiting maid, who watched the execution with great complaisance, told him afterwards that the poor girl was dead, or at least quite insensible to pain, long before the whipping was over. "Little fool to stay here when she might have gone with the other," concluded Gundruda.

"Fool indeed," said he, "I cannot forget it—I am not well, Gundruda, pretty one." She put her arms round him, and they strolled away together.

So Elgifu paid bitterly for her folly, and went to a rest which was denied her in this world.

In the early afternoon one of the men-at-arms, dressed as a peasant, set out for Icomb by water.

Lewin stayed with Gundruda a little while, trying to find comfort in her smiles and forgetfulness in her bright laughing eyes.

But the minter could find very little satisfaction with the girl. Her beauty and sprightly allurements had no appeal for him just then. There was no thrill even in her kisses. So after a while he left her, for a sudden longing to be alone came over him. The idea was strong in him to get as far away from the world as possible. By many steps he mounted to the top of Outfangthef. As he emerged into the light, after the dusk of the stairs, it began to be evening.

Down below, over all the castle works, men were busy at the defences, clustering on the walls like a swarm of flies. Presently, one by one, torches flared out, so that work might still go on when it was dark.

Lewin leaned over the parapet and surveyed the dusky world, full of trouble and despair. A great truth came to him. He realised that he had been born too soon, and was not made for that age of blood and steel. The solitary isolation of the tower top intensified the loneliness of his own soul.

Surveying life and its possibilities for him, he could see nothing but misery in it. As the unseen nightwinds began to fly round him and whisper, he took a resolve. When this siege began and Lord Roger attacked Hilgay, he would arm and go out to death, seeking it in some brave adventure. He would give up, he thought, his treason plot with Anselm. There was nothing else that he could do, there was no enjoyment—every man he knew was the same, the same, ever-lastingly the same. Life was dull. He laughed a bitter, despairing laugh, and went down to the castle again.

There was a great carouse that evening at Hilgay, for the works were nearly done, and a spy had brought word that the forces of Lord Roger were not as strong as earlier reports had led them to believe.

While the candles burnt all night by the grave in the chapel, all the castle garrison, with the exception of the sentries, got most gloriously drunk. Lewin was no exception.

It is a relief to turn from the contemplation of that sordid, evil place to the quiet of the Priory in the lake. Yet it must be remembered that Hilgay is an exact type of hundreds of other strongholds existing in England at that time. The incalculable wickedness of the space of years, when the secluded historian wrote that "Christ and all His angels seemed asleep," is very difficult to imagine.

In truth, it was a bestial, malignant, inhuman time. We are not grateful enough for the blessings of to-day. Imagine, if you please, what these people were.

There is no need to outrage our nice tastes by revolting detail. Realism can be pushed too far. But, for the sake of a clear understanding, take Baron Fulke of Hilgay, and listen to a few personal details.

The beast was a very well-bred man. That is to say, he was of the aristocracy, a peer with a great record of birth. We have seen that he stripped his mistress naked, and had her killed by rough scoundrels in his pay. He never had a qualm. So much for his character, which was as much like the legendary devil as may be. But about the man as a personality.

Supposing that we could draw a parallel between that time and our own time. Fulke would correspond to half a dozen young gentlemen we all know, considered from the point of view of social status. A boy we meet at a dance, or a dinner, who is a member of a great family, for example.

Fulke, unpleasant as it is to say it, *hardly ever washed.* Brutally, in a modern police court, he would be considered as a verminous person. In the time of King Stephen, no one—and we can make no exception for the saints of God themselves—had ever heard of a pocket handkerchief. The world was malodorous! A dog-kennel would hardly have suffered any one of our heroes and heroines, That is one reason why it is so difficult for the veracious historian to present his characters as they really were. It is hard to explain them, people are too accustomed to Romance.

There is hardly anything in our steam age so delightful as "Romance." The romance of the early Middle Ages has a quality of glamour which will hold our attention and have our hearts for ever. We always look for, and desire refinements of fact in life. Human nature demands some sort of an ideal. Our friends of the fens can hardly be called romantic, but they are human.

The Serf

While all these cut-throats were rioting in the keep, Richard Espec, the prior of Icomb, was sitting in his cell working.

A candle in an iron holder stood on the table by him, and threw a none too brilliant light upon a mass of documents. "Contrepaynes" of leaves, pages of accounts, and letters from brother churchmen.

At the moment, the prior was checking the accounts of the oil mill, which was a source of revenue to the house.

There came a knock at the door with a "Benedicite," the prior bid the knocker enter. The new-comer was the sub-prior, John Croxton, Richard Espec's great friend and counsellor.

"Sit down," said the prior, "and tell me the news—is there any news? I am very weary of figuring, and I feel sad at heart. Richard Cublery has paid no rent for a year and a half, since he fell to drinking heavily with John Tichkill."

"We can survive that," said the sub-prior.

"Yes, yes; I am not accoyed at that, brother, but the letters and tidings from the outside world oppress me. The various and manifold illegalities and imposts which never cease or fail on the wretched people, and the burnings and murders lie heavy on my heart. Oh, our Lord has some wise purpose, I do not doubt, but it is all very dark to mortal eyes."

"I have read," said the sub-prior, "somewhat of history in my time. But never in Latin times, nor can I hear of it of the Greeks, was there such a spirit of devilish wickedness abroad over a land."

"The lords of this country seem to me to be the daemons of hell in mortal dress. Mind you what Robert Belesme did? His godchild was hostage to him for its father, and the father did in some trifling way offend him. Robert tore out the poor little creature's eyes with his nails. William of Malmesbury hath writ it in his book, and, please God, the world will never forget it."

"The king has got to him all the worst rogues from over the seas. William of Ypres, Hervè of Lèon, and Alan of Duran, there are three pretty gentlemen! The king is no king. There are in England, so to speak, as many kings, or rather tyrants, as lords of castles."

"Well, one of them is gone," said Richard Espec, "and I trust God will forgive him, though I feel that it is not likely. He was one of the worst ones, was Geoffroi de la Bourne."

"That was he. For myself, I cannot even understand how a man can be as bad as that. A sinner, yes, and a bad one, but from our point of view, you and I, can you see yourself, even if you were not a monk, doing any of these things?"

"Without doubt, brother. Only an old man like I can really know how foul and black a thing the human heart is. Every one is a potential Geoffroi, save but for the grace of God, given for sweet Christ's sake."

"Yes, father," said the younger man, folding his arms meekly. The candles on the tables began to gutter towards their end, and throw monstrous shadows upon the faces and over the forms of the two monks. They were talking in low tones, and the little stone room was very silent. The dying candle-flames filled it with rich, velvety shadows, and dancing yellow lights.

"Hyla and his friends have been given the large hut that Swegn had before he died. I saw the meeting between him and his womenfolk. They hardly looked to see him again."

"I do not care much to have so many women about," said Richard, with the true monkish distrust of the other sex. "Nevertheless, the men can not be easily kept without their wives. And of this Hyla—what do you think of him?"

The Serf

"He seems a very strong nature for a serf. Singularly contained within himself, and, I think, proud of his revenge."

"That must not be, then. We must not let him be that. I well think that he has been chosen by God as His instrument, and for that I rejoice. But the man must not get proud. He is a serf, and a serf he will be always. It is in his blood, and it is right that it should be so. I am no upholder of any destruction of order. It is our duty to treat our slaves well, and that we do; but they remain our slaves. Tell the brother who directs the serfs that this Hyla should be well looked to, that he lie in his true place."

The prior concluded with considerable vehemence. No one was more theoretically conservative than he, and although, in this time of anarchy, he approved of Hyla's deed, yet it certainly shocked his instinctive respect for *les convenances*. It would have been difficult to find a better creature than the fat prior of Icomb, a man more truly charitable, or of a more pious life. But, had the course of this story been different, and had Hyla lived his life at the monastery, he could never have risen in the social scale. If the prior had discovered the force of the man, his potentialities as a social force, he would have sternly repressed them. Hyla's duty was to work, and be fed for his work. The Catholic Church, with its vast hierarchy, its huge social machinery, crushed all progress in the direction of freedom. No doubt, Richard Espec, worthy gentleman though he was, would have been considerably surprised if he had been told that he would be as Hyla, and no more, in heaven. We hear too much about the humility of the priesthood in the early Middle Ages. Of course, the great political churchmen, such as Henry of Winchester or Thurston of York, were petty kings, with ceremonial courts and armies. People knelt as they passed, because they were princes as well as priests. But there is a delusion that the ordinary monk or priest was, in effect, a perfect radical, holding doctrines of equality, at any rate, as far as he himself was concerned. Nothing of the sort was possible in the face of the one crushing social fact of serfdom. Richard Espec would have washed Hyla's feet with pleasure—there was precedent, and it was a formal act of humiliation. At the same time, he would not have made his bed in Hyla's hut or sat with him at meat.

The sub-prior received his superior's remarks with due reverence, and the talk glided into other channels. While they sat there came footsteps running down the cloister, and then a beating at the door. A young monk entered, breathless, and knelt before the prior.

"News, father," said he, and craved permission to tell it. "Father," said the young man, and tears streamed down his cheeks, "our good friend, Sir John Leyntwarden, is dead, and among the martyrs. Sir John was saying Mass at the wayside altar of Saint Alban, the protomartyr whom God loves. Sir John doth ever say a wayside Mass in the early mornings, and calls down a blessing upon the Norwich road thereby. Now the boy Louis Seèz was helping Sir John to serve the Mass, and his tale is this—Sir John had just divided the Host, and allowed the particle to fall into the chalice. Indeed, he was saying the *Haec commixtio*. Suddenly they heard a loud laugh, and so harsh was it in the holy stillness that verily Satan might have had just such a laugh. Father, thinking that it was indeed some daemon come out of the wood, Sir John started and turned round. There he saw five gentlemen on horseback and in armour. They had ridden up very quietly over the turf. Down the road, a mile away, Sir John saw a great company moving. He saw spears, and the sun on armour and waggons. He knew then that this was some great lord's war train, and that the gentlemen who were watching him had ridden on before."

The young monk stopped a moment for lack of breath and labouring under great agitation. The other two gazed intently at him in great excitement. Sir John Leyntwarden, the priest of Hawle, was their very good friend, and a holy man. The news was horrible.

"Calm, brother," said the prior, "say an *Ave* and pray a moment, peace will come to you then."

The Serf

The curious remedy served its turn wonderfully well—wherefore let no man smile at Richard Espec—and the young monk resumed his narrative.

"Then said Sir John to the gentlemen, 'Sirs, the *Agnus Dei* is not yet, and there is time for you to kneel and take our Lord's Body with us. *Vere dignum et justum est aequum et salutare.* Then the leader of the party, a powerful, great man, laughed again. Louis says it was verily like a devil mocking, for it was very bitter, mirthless, and cold. This lord said, 'We take no Mass, but, by hell, we will have these thy vessels. They are too good for a hedge priest.' Then he did turn to a lady who sat by upon a white horse, very dark, and with white teeth which laughed. 'What Kateryn?' said he. 'They will make thee a drinking-cup and a plate until I can give thee better from the cellars of Hilgay.' Then Louis knew who it was. That was my Lord Roger Bigot with Kateryn Larose, his concubine, and the war train was on its way to Hilgay Tower to overthrow Fulke de la Bourne.

"Sir John held up the cross at his girdle and dared them that they should come nearer to the Body of Christ. The harlot in the saddle kissed her fingers to him, and the whole company laughed. Then, with no more ado, they took him and bound him. In the melley little Louis slipped away, and the grievous things which happened he saw from a tree hard by. They emptied the chalice and pyx upon the ground. 'Look,' said Lord Roger, 'there is your God, Sir Priest, and thus I treat Him.' With that a-stamped upon the Host, and all the company laughed at that awful crime."

Richard Espec and John Croxton burst into loud cries of pity and horror at this point. Tears rained down the prior's face as he heard how these evil men had entreated the Body and Blood.

"Louis thought to see heaven open and Abdiel drop from the morning sky, like fire, to kill them. But God made no sign.

"Then Sir John, lying bound upon the ground, began to pray in a loud voice that God would terribly punish these men. He called upon them the curse of all the Saints, and he said to Roger Bigot that for this deed he should lie for ever in hell. There was something strange about his voice, or perhaps they were frightened at the curses. Roger ground his mailed heel into Sir John's face till it was no face and he was silent. Then for near half-an-hour they did torture him with terrible tortures, and with one unspeakable. You know, father, in what manner the saints have suffered that have fallen into the hands of Robert, or Roger, or Geoffroi. Sir John could not abear it, and he screamed loudly till his voice rang through all the wood. So died dear Sir John in the fresh morning."

Richard Espec made the sign of the cross, and said solemnly, "*Posuisti, Domine, super caput ejus, coronam de lapide pretioso. Alleluia.*" Then he said, "Go and summon all the brethren to the chapter-house, for I have somewhat to say to them." And being left alone he fell upon his knees in prayer.

The great bell in the centralone began to toll loudly.

This dreadful news touched the prior very nearly. Dom Leyntwarden, the vicar of Hawle-in-the-wood, a tiny hamlet now deserted, was an intimate and close friend of his. The murdered priest was a shrewd adviser upon business affairs, and would often come over to the monastery and be its guest for a few days, to help in any worldly business that might be afoot. He was endeared to the whole Priory. It was a terrible instance of the times in which they lived. The good priest saying Mass at the little wayside altar by the wood in the fresh morning air. The sneering, relentless fiends in mail, and the smiling girl upon her palfrey. In one short hour their friend had passed from them in agony, from the real presence of God into the real presence of God made manifest to his eyes.

The prior was resolved to address the assembled brethren in the chapter-house, not one being absent.

We are enabled to see how all this bore upon the fortunes of Hyla.

Sir John Leyntwarden was martyred by Roger Bigot on his way to attack Hilgay.

Sir John was a friend of the monks with whom Hyla had taken refuge. On the occasion of the news the prior summoned a chapter of the brethren, and all the men living in the monastery village on the hill who were not serfs.

The village was practically empty and free to the hands of a long boat of armed men, which, under cover of the dark, was now moving swiftly over the lake.

CHAPTER IX

"Justorum Animae in Manu dei sunt, et non Tanget Illos Tormentum Malitiae: Visi sunt Oculis Insipientium Mori, Illi Autem sunt in Pace."

The chapter-house at Icomb was a low, vaulted chamber divided into three compartments by rows of pillars bearing arches. A stone seat ran all round it for the monks, and the prior's seat was opposite the entrance. Two arches on each side of the doorway—there was no actual door—allowed the deliberations to be heard outside in the cloister. This was according to the invariable Cistercian plan. No one, save the monks themselves, could actually sit in the chapter-house, but others—in this case, the head men of the village—could stand in the cloister, and so become fully cognisant of the proceedings within.

The brothers filed through the dark cloisters towards the red doorways which showed that the chapter-house was lit within. The big bell in the centralone kept tolling unceasingly. One by one the brothers entered and seated themselves upon the stone bench. Two of the *fratres conversi* stood by the prior's throne with torches. A sudden murmur of talk hummed through the place. The night was exceedingly hot.

A glance round at the seated figures would hardly have prepossessed the modern spectator. One and all, young and old, were as frowsy and unsavoury a lot as ever poisoned the air of a warm summer's night. The white, emaciated faces smeared with dirt, the matted beards, and glowing, excited eyes, all combined to produce a singularly unpleasant picture.

Yet as the torchlight revealed one distressing detail after another it also played upon a congregation of as holy men as could have been found anywhere in that century. Not for them the licence and luxury of some of the great monasteries, where the monks pursued the deer or set their falcons at feathered game with no less ardour than they followed a petticoat through a wood. Not for them chased cups of pimentum and morat while the tables groaned under fish, flesh and fowl. It is a pity, no doubt, that they were not nice according to our ideas, but we can well forget that if we remember that they were indeed very holy men.

Presently the prior came in and took his seat upon the stone throne after he had said a short Latin prayer. The farmers and other villagers pressed to the archways of the opening, and, rising to his feet, Richard Espec spake in this wise:

"Brethren, this is a perilous time; and such a scourge was never heard since Christ's passion. You hear how good men suffer the death. Brethren, this is undoubted for the offences of England. Ye read, as long as the children of Israel kept the commandments of God, so long their enemies had no power over them, but God took vengeance of their enemies. We have erred, I wist, in our own lives, and God has sent this upon us. For when the Jews broke God's commandments then they were subdued by their enemies, and so be we. Therefore let us be sorry for our offences. Undoubted He will take vengeance of our enemies; I mean those blood-stained lords that causeth so many good men to suffer thus. Alas! it is a piteous case that so much Christian blood should be shed. Therefore, good brethren, for the reverence of God, every one of you devoutly pray, and say this psalm, 'O God, the heathen are come into Thine inheritance; Thy holy temple have they defiled, and made Jerusalem a heap of stones. The dead bodies of Thy servants have they given to be meat to the fowls of the air, and the flesh of Thy saints unto the beasts of the field. Their blood have they shed like water on every side of Jerusalem, and there was no man to bury them. We are become an open scorn to our enemies, a very scorn and derision to them that are round about us. Oh, remember not our old sins, but have mercy upon us, and that soon, for we are come to great misery. Help us, O God of our salvation, for the glory of Thy name. Oh, be merciful unto our sins for Thy name's sake. Wherefore do the heathen say, Where is now their God?' Ye shall say this psalm," continued the prior, "every Friday, after the Litany, prostrate, when ye lie upon the high altar, and undoubtedly God will cease this extreme scourge."

Then he went on to tell them of the martyrdom of Dom John, and what a good and holy man he was. "Even now, my dear brethren," said he, "I know him to be a saint in heaven. *He has seen God*, and talked with His Holiness, Saint Peter. Our Lady has smiled upon him. In the golden streets he has walked with gladness. I think that perhaps he is here with us now, our dear brother, that he sees us, and is full of love towards us all."

As his voice dropped towards the close, full of emotion, there was loud applause. As in very early Christian times, the brethren saluted the oration with a beating of hands.

And with that noise we must leave the hooded figures sitting among the shadows.

The curtain of this short chronicle must fall upon them for ever, in a red light, with black shadows, with the noise of a clapping of hands.

Their lives were framed in stone, and swords were about them. They were very ignorant, very prejudiced, superstitious and dirty—a big indictment! Nevertheless, it is certain that their influence upon the time was good and pure. It is the fashion to rail at monasteries of all periods. Many blockheads can never get over the mere *fact* of the Dissolution! In a spirit of curiosity I examined half-a-dozen histories of the baser type— the sort of histories that are still given to fourth-form boys and quite grown-up girls. One and all, if they mentioned the monasteries in the reign of King Stephen at any length, either openly condemned them or damned them with faint praise. I take this opportunity of correcting messires, the historians, upon a point of FACT. It is odd that the hopelessly incompetent clergyman-schoolmaster should so invariably turn historian to-day. His monumental and appalling ignorance of the times and peoples he treats of—ignorance unillumined with a single ray of insight—is displayed on every line of his lucubrations. Nothing, apparently, would lead him to read and dig and sift for himself so that he might know just a little of what he writes about. Let me, at any rate, assure him, that while, as is natural, there were plenty of bad monks in the reign of Stephen, as a whole, the monasteries were very praiseworthy institutions, and had a beneficent influence upon the country. In short, my little priory at Icomb, is a perfectly fair and typical example of its class.

While the monks were in the chapter-house, and afterwards attending a special service in the chapel, a long boat glided rapidly over the lake. It was a dark, thunderous night, and nothing betrayed the quiet passage of the craft, save the dusky glitter of the water as the oars rose and sank. Now and again some low orders in Norman-French regulated the pace or altered the direction of the boat.

When the voyagers were about half-way across the mere, as near as they could judge, they heard the sudden tolling of the great bell of the Priory. The sullen, angry notes came across the water, out of the dark, in waves of booming sound. There was a muttered order, and the oars stopped in their swing. The boat rushed on for thirty yards or so, gradually losing its momentum, until at length it became stationary.

"What does that betoken, Huber?" asked a voice.

"I do not know," replied the man-at-arms. "Pardieu, I cannot tell."

"Do you think they know that we are near?"

"Not unless they have found out that Heraud has come with a certain purpose. Perchance Hyla saw him and recognised him."

"Not he. Heraud shaved his face and cropped his hair, and the minter drew lines upon his face, and painted the poor divell's visage all over with some hell brew. I seed them at it. His own mother would never have thought him made of her blood."

"Then, by Godis teeth! what does the bell mean?"

"Oh, the old women are making prayers or saying Mass."

"Pagan! Mass is not at this hour, nor would they ring the great bell in that way."

"Then the prior has given up his vows, and is about to wed the Lady Abbess of Denton, and the monks are ringing for joy that one of them should at length prove himself a man." A chuckle went through the boat at this none too excellent a joke.

"Like enough," Huber said, "but whatever it may mean we must keep our tryst with Heraud. It was to be a church's length from the main landing where the monks keep their boats. A church's length to the left."

"It will not be easy to find, the night is very thick. We must go very slow."

"Yes," said Huber "we must go with great care. Come forward! Are you ready? Allery!"

The boat glided slowly on again towards the direction of the island. Presently a deeper blackness loomed up in front of them, and they saw that they were close to land. The smell of land, of herbage and flowers, came to them, and hot as it had been upon the lake, it seemed hotter now that they were come to shore.

As the nose of the boat brushed the outgrowing reeds, hissing at the contact, the bell on the hill above stopped suddenly. A great silence enveloped them as they waited.

Huber gave a long, low whistle, but there was no answer. He repeated it at intervals of about a minute.

They were getting restive, wondering what might have happened, when Huber changed his tactics. He began to whistle very softly and sweetly—the scamp had a pipe like any bird—the lilt of a love-song. It was a plaintive air which rose and fell delicately in the night. Most of them knew it, for it was a popular song among the soldiers of that day, and had been made by a strolling minstrel one evening in the Picard camp at Gournay, and thence spread all over Northern Europe by the mercenaries.

The men-at-arms began to nod to its rhythm and beat quiet time to it. Then one fellow began to whistle a bass under his breath, and another and another took up the air very quietly, till the boat was like a cage of fairy singing birds. They were so amused by their occupation, and, indeed, they were producing a very pretty concert, that they quite forgot their purpose for the moment, and abandoned themselves one and all to the music. It recalled many merry memories of Tilliers and Falaise, of Mortain and Arques, and of the orchards of their Norman home.

They were beginning the whole thing all over again—so much did it please them—when they became aware of another and more distant augmentation to their concert. They stopped, and the silvery whistle from the bank still shivered out a note or two before it stopped. In a moment more they heard splashing, and a dark figure pushed aside the reeds and waded out to them.

The Serf

"It is all safe," said the new-comer. "The murderer is here sure enough. He does not know who I am, and I am in a hut close to his."

"Bon," said Huber, "I am glad to see you. Lord Fulke will be very pleased. We feared something was wrong when we heard the bell."

"Depardieux! and well you might. I did not think of that. But natheless, that bell means good fortune for our little plan, my friends. All the monks and all the villeins from the village have gone inside to service in the chapel. Only the theows are alone, and it will be an easy matter to take the man without interference if we are quick."

"How far is it from here?"

"As a bird flies, about two furlongs. But it will be longer for us, for we must make a detour to keep away from the walls. We shall come on the village from behind. There is a big midden ditch, but I have a plank to cross it."

"We'll give Sir Hyla a dip in it as we pass."

"'Twould be a fitting mitra."

Then with no more words, led by Heraud, they left the boat and stole silently up the hill in the dark.

An archer remained in the boat to guard it and to help them to find it again.

Hyla retired into his hut about half-past eight. He had been working all day, cleaning out pig-styes and carting the manure to the ditch which ran north of the village, and which served as a slight defence, and also as a storing place for fertilizing material to spread upon the fields. A strange occupation, perhaps, for a man who had but lately done a deed of such moment, and who was more than half a hero! But he had been set to this work purposely by the monks, who knew human nature, and thought it best for the man. The monks were the only psychologists in the twelfth century.

With some men this would have been wise, no doubt, but to Hyla's credit it should be said that he thought very little about himself. His rather heavy, sullen manner may easily have conveyed a false impression as to his own estimate of himself, but he was humble enough in reality.

In fact, Hyla was too humble, and more so than befitted his strong nature. He cleaned the filth from the styes with never a thought that he might be better or more profitably employed. And in this fact we have another vivid expression of the psychology of serfdom.

The only certain way in which it is possible to get at the inner meaning of a period in history, is by the comparison of the attitude of an individual brain towards his time, and the attitude of a general type of brain. The individual with the point of view must, of course, be a known quantity.

Historians, I am certain, have not yet entirely realised this simple and beautiful method. Properly understood, it is as mathematically exact as any comparative method can possibly be. It is the way in which history will be written in the future when the modern Headmaster-Historian will no longer be allowed to write an "epoch" and dispose of the two first editions entirely among the boys of his own school.

Of its extreme fascination as a pursuit the cultured cannot speak too highly. It combines the pleasures of the laboratory with the pleasures of psychology, and never was Science so happily wedded to Art.

Here is a trifling case in point. Friend Hyla—whose temperament we know something of—felt no degradation in cleaning out the pig-stye, although he had just done a great and noble thing. We know Hyla as a man very far from perfect. We know him subject to the ordinary failings of mankind. Why, then, was Hyla content? The answer supplies us with

The Serf

a luminous exposition of serfdom as a social state, how stern a thing it was, how bitter. Pages of rhetoric could give no better explanation of that hard fact.

So Hyla had been quite content, and as the sun was setting he sat down outside his hut with his wife on one side and his daughter on the other, as happy as a man could be. Bread and meat lay upon the ground by his side. A cow's horn full of Welsh ale was stuck into the turf by him. He was now working for kind masters who would not beat him or ill-treat his womankind. His hut was weather-proof, his food was excellent, and the peace of the holy life near by was stealing over him, and he was at last at rest. The peace of it all was like a cup of cold water to a poor man dying of thirst.

He stroked his wife's hard gnarled hand, very glad to be so close to her. He looked with unconscious admiration at the frank beauty of Frija as she lay gracefully by his side. Only one grief assailed him now, and that was the thought of Elgifu. He put it from him with a shudder. Yet, he thought, they would hardly hurt her. He was a man of bitter experience, and felt that she would be fairly safe in that wicked time.

Before the little family retired to rest, Cerdic came to them to pray. The ex-lawer of dogs had, it must be confessed, most of the instincts of the street-corner preacher. He was never so happy as when he was making an extempore prayer, and in his heart of hearts he felt sure that he should have been a priest. Hyla regarded this accomplishment of his friend's with unfeigned admiration. Cerdic's praying was his one great pleasure. Both men were perfectly sincere about it. Cerdic and Hyla were both quite certain that the Saints heard and remarked upon every word. At the same time, in an age when music was a monopoly, literature a thing for the fortunate few, and the theatre was not, these poor fellows found their æsthetic excitement in family prayers. Indeed, if we come to think of it, the Puritan classes in England to-day are much the same. Indeed, as long as the saving grace of Sincerity is present, the plan seems excellent. It will not fill the pockets of the theatrical manager, but it will keep a good many fools out of mischief.

So, with full bellies and in great peace of mind, Hyla and Cerdic prayed to God, and fell upon sleep.

Another hour of peaceful sleep remains for you, poor Hyla. Another little hour, and then good-bye to sleep. Good-bye to wife and child and comfort for ever and a day. A few short hours and you go to the beginning of your great martyrdom. Your works shall live after you.

But hush! the time is nearly gone, the sands are running very rapid in the glass. Sleep has still a gift for you, lie undisturbed!

CHAPTER X

"At the sight therefore, of this river, the Pilgrims were much stunned; but the men that went with them said, 'You must go through, or you cannot come at the gate.'"

Hyla slept ill after an hour or two. Tired nature gave him a physical oblivion for a time, but when his exhaustion was worked off, he began to toss uneasily and to dream. The events of the past days danced in a confused jumble in his brain, and the dominant sensation was one of gliding over water.

Water and the vast lonely fen lands were vividly before him in a hundred uneasy and fantastic ways. He awoke to find the hut hot and stifling beyond all bearing. The deep breathing of his women folk was all the immediate sound he heard, though an owl was sobbing intermittently in the wood by the lake.

How hot it was! The rich earthy smell, a fertile, luxuriant odour of life, was terribly oppressive. There was an earthen jar of lake water at the door of the hut, but when he groped a silent way to it, he found it warm and full of the taste of weeds and tree roots. There was no comfort in it.

He stood looking out into the night. There was no moon, but it was hardly dark. Now and then a ghostly sheet of summer lightning flickered over the sky. Late as it was the air was full of flying insects. The cockchafers boomed as they circled over the enclosure in their long, swift flight. Great moths, with huge fat bodies, hung on the roofs of the huts or flapped to the neighbouring trees. The heavy, lazy Goat Moths, three years old, and nearly four inches from wing to wing. The male Wood Leopard, more active than his great brother, the sombre-coloured Noctuas, the evil-looking, long-bodied Hawk Moths, all danced in the dusky air.

Out in the fields the crickets sang like a thousand little bells, and the atropus, a tiny insect from which bucolic superstition has evolved the "death watch," ticked as it ran over the door posts.

Glow-worms winked in pale gleams among the grass, and louder than any other noise was the deep hum of the great Stag-beetle as he flew by. A myriad night life pulsed round the waking man. The Goatsucker flew round the borders of the wood catching the insects in his flight, and his strange, jarring pipe thrilled all the heavy air; among the leaves and undergrowth the Hedgepig, rested with his long day's sleep, rustled in search of food, making his curious, low, gurgling sound, and rattling his spines.

In those far-off days wild life luxuriated and throve. Day and night were full of strange sounds heard but rarely now. As Hyla stood wearily by his hut, the Polecat was fishing for eels in the mud of the lake shore. Old dog-foxes slunk through the woods in search of prey, while their cubs frisked like kittens in the open spaces of the woods, playing hide-and-seek, and engaging in a mimic warfare. The air was full of Noctules and Natterers, great silent bats.

In some dim way, Hyla was influenced by all this vitality around him. Richard Espec in his place would have said, "In wisdom Thou hast made them all, the earth is full of Thy riches. Thou openest Thy hand and fillest all things living with plenteousness; they continue this day according to Thine ordinance, for all things serve Thee. He spake the word and they were made, He commanded, and they were created!"

That would have been the logical expression of a good man who spent his life in reconciling the concrete with the unseen. Hyla's attitude was just the same, though he was not educated to elevate a thought into an expression of thought.

But, nevertheless, he felt the mystery of the night, and the live creatures at work in it.

The Spirit of God worked in him as it worked in wiser and more considerable men.

But it was rather lonely also. His great deed still had its influence of terror upon him. A man who violently disturbs the society in which he lives and moves, as Hyla had done, wants human companionship. It is ill to know one is absolutely alone.

He thought that he would seek Cerdic, if, perchance, he was in a mood for talk, and not too drowsy. He went towards his friend's hut. In the dim light, as he threaded his way across the stoke, he saw that many other serfs had found their shelters too noisesome and hot for comfort. They lay about in front of the huts in curious twisted attitudes, breathing heavily with weariness and sleep.

Cerdic had also chosen the air to lie in. He was stretched on a skin, lying on his back, and in his hand was a half-eaten piece of black bread, showing that sleep had caught him before he had finished his supper.

Hyla lent over him and whispered in his ear. It was interesting to see how quickly and yet how silently the man awoke. With no sound of astonishment or surprise, he sat up, with alert enquiring eyes, full awake and ready for anything that might be toward.

The Serf

"Peace!" said Hyla, "there is nothing to trouble about. But I cannot sleep, and feel very lonely, and want speech with a man. The air is full of winged things, and the shaw yonder of beasts. I do not know why, I want a man's voice."

"You made your bede to-night?" said Cerdic.

"Yes, I prayed, Cerdic, and you with me. But I feel ill at ease, and sweating with the heat."

"Yes, yes," said Cerdic, as one who was used to these fleeting sicknesses of the brain, and as one who could prescribe a cure. "I wist well how you feel, Hyla. 'Tis the night and the loneliness of it. Onnethe can a man be alone at night unless he is busy upon something. Come sit you down and talk."

They reclined side by side upon the grass, but neither had much to say. Hyla found something comforting in the companionship of Cerdic.

"I keep minding *His* face," said Hyla suddenly.

"Then you are a fool, Hyla. But I wist that is only because 'tis night-time. You are not troubled in the day. You have had your wreak upon your foe. Let it be, it is done, and Sir Priest hath absolved you from sin, and eke me."

He looked at Hyla with a smile, as who should say that the argument was irresistible.

"Cerdic," said Hyla, "I feel in truth something I cannot say. I am absolved and stainless, I wist well, yet I am accoyed. I fear some evil, and the night is strange. The air is thick with flies and such volatile, and—I wist not. I wist not what I mean."

"Hast eaten too heavily and art troubled by this new place. Shall I pray for you a space?"

His face lit up with eagerness as he said it.

"Not now, Cerdic," said Hyla, "I am not for bede to-night. Come you with me to lake-side; there will be air upon the water, perchance. I cannot breathe here."

"I have slept enough and will go with you, but these sick fancies are not in your fashion. You have never been y-wone to them; and for my part, Hyla, I put my trust in my lords the angels, and think that evil thoughts come from devils of Belsabubbis line."

Hyla crossed himself in silence. "Rest a moment," he said. "I will see if Gruach wakes, and if she does, tell her I am going to the lake-side for coolness, and that I cannot sleep."

But when he got to the hut it was as silent as when he had left it, and he heard the untroubled breathing of the women he loved.

With a curious expression of tenderness for so outwardly unemotional a man he made the sign of salvation in the gloom of the door, and with a heart full of foreboding turned towards Cerdic.

The lawer-of-dogs was not anxious to leave his sleep and wander through the night. Far rather would he have lain sleeping till the sun and birds of morning called him to work in a happy security he had never known before. But there was a great loyalty in him, and a love for his friend that was as sincere as it was unspoken.

Moreover, he began to see of late new traits in Hyla. He found him changed and less easily understood. Mental influences seemed at work in him which raised him, or removed him, from the ordinary men Cerdic knew. Cerdic only *felt* this. He did not think it. Yet his unconscious realisation of the fact made him defer to Hyla's moods and fall in with his suggestion.

He was a shrewd, gentle, fine-natured man. I should like to have clasped his hand.

He put a lean, brown paw on Hyla's broad shoulder, and together they threw the plank over the evil-smelling ditch, malodorous and poisoning the night, and strode out into the wood.

The Serf

They flitted noiselessly among the dark trees, silent amid the noble aisles and avenues which sloped down to the lake.

The air was certainly cooler as they left the stoke behind.

They had gone some distance upon their way when they sat for a moment to rest upon the bole of a fallen oak tree in a little open glade some ten yards square. The clearing was fairly light, but a black wall of trees encompassed it. There, such was the influence of the place and hour, they fell talking of abstractions with as much right and probably as luminous a point of view as their betters.

"What think you, lad, Geoffroi be doing now?" said Hyla.

"Burning in hellis fire," said Cerdic in a tone of absolute conviction.

"Think you for ever?" said Hyla musingly.

"Aye, Hyla, I pray Our Lady. The Saints would not have him in heaven, and I wist St. Jesu also."

"We might go to him," said Hyla.

Cerdic gazed at him through the dark with genuine astonishment.

"By Godis ore!" he said, "never shall we two roast for long. Prior hath prayed with us and we are shriven. We have done no man harm. I am certain, Hyla, that the Saints and Our Lady will take us in. An it only be to carry water or dung fields, we shall be taken in."

The absolute assurance in his tone told upon the other and comforted him.

"Art not accoyed to die?" he asked.

"No wit. Natheless, I would live a little longer now we have won kind masters. Yet would I die this night withouten fear. I would well like to see the Blessed Lady and all her train. It will be a wonderful fine sight, Hyla."

As they sat thus, talking simply of that other life, which was so real to them in their childlike, undisturbed faith, they did not hear the moving of many feet through the underwood or the low whispers of a body of men who were approaching the glade in which they sat.

One loud word, a chance oath, would have startled them away and saved them. Indeed, had they not been so intent upon high matters they must have heard footsteps. Trained foresters as they were, creatures of the fields, the woods, and the open heavens, no men were more quick to hear the advance of any living thing or more prompt to avoid hostile comers.

The first intimation that came to them was the sudden clank of a steel-headed pike as it fell and rattled against a tree stump. They leapt to their feet, but it was too late. The wood seemed peopled with armed men. Their alarm came upon them so quickly that each tree all round was transformed into a man-at-arms. Before they could turn to fly the leaders of the band were up with them, and strong mailed arms grasped them.

Black-bearded faces peered into theirs, striving to see who they were in that dim light.

"Are ye prior's men?" said Huber, in a low, eager voice.

Then with a sick fear the two serfs knew into whose hands they had fallen. With an icy chill of despair, they realised that these were Fulke's men, and that his vengeance was long-armed, and had come upon them stealthily in the night.

Then in that moment of anguish, they tasted all the bitterness of death. The new, fair life that was opening before them so brightly vanished in a flash. The old cruel voices of their masters were like heavy chains; a black curtain fell desolately and finally over their lives.

Suddenly one of the men who had been scrutinising them closely gave a loud and joyous cry. "God's rood!" he shouted. "These be the two men themselves a-coming to meet with us in t' wood! Mordieu, these be the murderers!"

The men-at-arms crowded round the captives with cries of savage joy. "The Saints have done this," cried one man. Then, being above all things soldiers, and alive to all the fortunes and chances which await men in a hostile neighbourhood, they bound the serfs with thongs, and hurried them swiftly down the hill to the boat.

CHAPTER XI

"Roweth on fast! who that is faint
In evil water may he be dreynt!"
They rowed hard and sung thereto
With hevelow and rumbeloo.

The boat glided through the reeds and hissed among the stalks as it floated off into deep water.

The man-at-arms who had been pushing it scrambled over the flat stern drenched to his waist.

Hyla and Cerdic lay bound where they had been flung at the bottom of the boat as roughly and carelessly as sacks of meal.

They moved slowly over the deep black waters. "The priests'll wake to find the pies flown," said Huber, emphasising his remark with a lusty kick upon the prostrate Cerdic.

"What will they think?" asked some one.

"I neither know eke care. Perchance it will be thought the divill has took them to his own place."

"Whence they will shortly go."

"Not before they have tasted of hell in Hilgay," and the speaker went on to enumerate with much spirit and vividness the several tortures to which the captives would be subjected before Death was merciful.

That these were no idle boasts to frighten them Cerdic and Hyla were very well aware. They had seen with their own eyes how men were punished for a far less offence than theirs. Nameless atrocities were committed upon the serfs, and the mocking words of the soldier had a terrible significance for them. The boat moved but very slowly. It was heavy, and the men were all tired out. Moreover, the night was oppressively hot even out upon the water.

Most of the rowers stripped to the waist and flung their garments down into the bottom of the boat. Hyla and Cerdic were covered with heavy, evil-smelling garments, and almost suffocated.

"I cannot breathe," whispered Hyla to Cerdic.

"Hist, listen! Get thy head down lower. Yes, so. Feel you my hands and the thong. There now; bite till I am free and can get at my dog-knife. God be praised, they did not see it!"

With a sudden leaping of his heart, forgetting the awful heat, Hyla cautiously lowered his head and began to nibble at the thong with strong, sharp teeth.

He could hear the muffled notes of an old Norman-French ballad telling of the nimbleness of Taillefer, as they sang to help the oars along.

"L'un dit á l'altre ki co veit

Ke co esteit enchantement,

Ke cil fesait devant la gent,"

and so forth, the doggerel sounding very melodious as the blended voices sent it out over the water.

The singing was an aid to their work, for it took away the attention of their guards. The greasy strap for a time resisted all his efforts. His teeth slid over the slippery surface and could not pierce it. Once there was a sharp crack, a twinge of pain, and a tooth broke in two. He was dismayed for a moment, but soon found the accident helped him.

The jagged edge of the broken bone soon made an incision in the leather, and with considerable pain he severed it at last.

The relief to Cerdic was extreme. They had tied his wrists so tightly that the thongs had cut deep into the flesh. For a moment or two his hands were quite lifeless and he could not move them. Then as the blood came flowing back into the stiffened fingers, pricking as though it were full of powdered glass, his mind also began to recover from its torpor and fear. He became alert, and his thoughts moved rapidly. He reached down cautiously for his knife and, inch by inch, withdrew it from the sheath. The jerkins which covered him were so thickly spread that more vigorous movements could hardly have been seen, but he trusted nothing to chance.

Soon Hyla's hands were free, and the thongs binding his ankles severed. They began to whisper a plan of escape.

Hyla was a good swimmer, and Cerdic a poor one, but death in the lake or the deep fen pools was far better than death with all the hideousness that would attend it at Hilgay Castle. The plan was this: When the men rested for a morning meal, which, they calculated would be at sunrise, they would make a sudden dash for freedom. By that time the lake would have been traversed, and the boat slowly threading the mazy water-ways of the fen. It would go hard with them if they could not get away from the heavily clad men-at-arms, all unused as they were to the country.

Meanwhile the rowers had got three parts of the way over the water. The sky was quite light now, with that cold grey-green which lasts for a few minutes before the actual sunrise.

"Sun will soon rise," said Heraud; "it's colder now, I will put on my jerkin."

"And I also," said several others, and the pile of clothes began to be lifted from the serfs.

It was a terribly anxious moment for them. If it was seen that bonds were cut, then they must risk everything, and jump into the lake, for they knew the boat could not have won the fen as yet.

Once in the lake their chance was small, unless it might happen that they were near the reeds which bordered it, and could swim to them and be lost in the fen. The boat could go far more swiftly than they could swim. In all probability there were cross-bows in it; they would be hunted through the water like drowning puppies.

One by one the rowers, chilled by their exertions, lifted the heavy leather garments from the two men. Cerdic continued to push his knife under him, and both men lay upon their stomachs, with their hands placed in the position they would have occupied had the thongs remained uncut.

Fortune was kind to them. When they at length lay bare to view, and the cold air came gratefully to their sweating bodies, the soldiers saw nothing. Heraud was the last man to take his coat, and he smote the back of Hyla's head heavily with his clenched fist.

The sudden pain and the foul words which accompanied the blow made the prostrate man quiver with rage. For a moment an impulse to fly at the throat of the man-at-arms,

The Serf

and risk everything in one wild exultation of combat, shook him through and through. He quivered with hatred and desire. But a low sibilant warning from Cerdic kept him fast, and with a mighty effort he restrained his passion.

Somewhat to the dismay of the serfs, the boat was stopped, and the soldiers produced food and beer from a basket and began to make a meal. Although they did not dare raise their heads to see, Cerdic and Hyla could hear from the talk of the men above them that they were yet a good half mile or more from the fen. The air began to grow a little warmer, and the sky to be painted in long crimson and golden streaks towards the East. Above their heads the heavy beating of great wings told them that the huge wild fowl of the fen were clanging out over the marshes for food.

Suddenly one of the soldiers, who was in the article of raising an apple to his mouth, began to snigger with amusement. The others followed the direction of his extended finger with their glance. He was pointing at Heraud. "Well, Joculator," snarled that worthy, "what be you a-mouthing at me for?"

"It's your face, Heraud," spluttered Huber. "By St Simoun, but I never thought of it till now. Should'st have washed it off!"

"Pardieu!" said Heraud "it be the minter's paint which I had forgot. A mis-begotten wretch I must look and no lesing! I will to the water and wash me like a Christian."

The man presented a curious and laughable appearance. Lewin had disguised him well, so that he might spy out where Hyla lay, but the exertion of rowing had induced perspiration, and the dusky colouring and painted eyebrows trickled down his hot, tired face in streaks. A black stubble of newly sprouting beard and moustache added to the comic effect.

"Ne'er did I see such a figure of fun as thou art, comrade!" said Huber in an ecstasy of mirth.

"Then, by Godis rood, I will make me clean," said Heraud good-humouredly. With that he got him to the boatside, and leaning over the gunwale began to lave himself vigorously in the fresh water.

In an earlier part of this book occurs a passage which is at some little trouble to explain that these men-at-arms were little more than ferocious unthinking children. The kneeling man presented a mark not only for quips of tongue but for a rougher and more physical wit. With a meaning wink at the others, John Pikeman withdrew a tholepin, about a foot long, from its socket, and with that stick did give Heraud a most sounding thwack upon the most exposed part of him.

With a sudden yell the unlucky wretch, as might have been foreseen, threw up his legs, and, with a loud gurgle, disappeared into the water. Now to these men, water was a thing somewhat out of experience. Not one in a hundred of them could swim; they were seldom put in the way of it, and a lake or river presented far more terrors to them than any walled town or field of battle.

The fact induces a reflection. Courage is purely relative. All of us can be brave in dangers we know, few of us but are not cowed in perils which are new. Poor Heraud was a striking example of the sententious truth. He rose choking, and his face was so white with fear, his eyes so pleading, his strong arms beat the water in such agony, that every rough heart in that boat was filled with anguish.

With one accord they rushed to the side of the boat, and immediately the inevitable happened.

The gunwale sank lower and lower, the cruel lip of black water rose hungrily to meet it, there was a sound like a man swallowing oil, a swirl, a rush of black water creamed into foam at its edge, and with a loud shout of dismay and terror the whole crew were struggling furiously in the water.

In a second the overturned boat had drifted yards away, and only the slimy green bottom projected above the flood.

Hyla and Cerdic, not being at the side of the boat, were not flung some distance out by the force of its turning, but sank together directly beneath it.

They rose almost at once, and both received smart knocks on the head from the timber. With little difficulty they dived and came up by the boat side. Each put a hand upon the slippery curved timbers, only obtaining a rest for the tips of the fingers, and, treading water, looked towards the drowning crowd a few yards away. The water was lashed into foam, as if some huge fish were disporting itself upon the surface. Heads kept bobbing up like corks, and sinking with a gurgling noise. Now and then a hand rose clutching the air in a death convulsion.

Amid all the confusion and tumult the wicker basket, which had held food, floated serenely, and the oars clustered round about it.

Every second, with a long groan, some sturdy fellow would catch at an oar end, the water pouring from his mouth and dripping from his cap. The thin pole would tip up with a jerk, and he would sink gurgling and coughing to his death. Meanwhile the sun came up the sky with one red stride, and illumined all the waters. The day broke cool and glorious, while these were dying. The day broke as it had done a thousand years before, and will a thousand years after you and I have sunk from one life and risen in another. Calm, glorious, unheeding, the sun rose over the waters, smiling inscrutably on those who were to know its secret so very soon.

In a few moments it was nearly over. Three heads remained above the water, as the serfs watched in fear. Huber swam round and round the other two, shouting directions and advice. One was Heraud, the other Jame, a cut-throat dog of no value. Both had but a few strokes, and their strength was failing fast.

The two heads sank lower and lower, the chins were submerged, the red line of the lips for a moment rested in line with the water, and then, with no sign or cry, they sank gently out of sight. Bubbles came up to the surface from a ten-yard circle, burst, and disappeared, the last sign that ten good fighting men were sinking asleep, deep down in the mud below.

As he saw his last two comrades go to their death, Huber gave a loud despairing cry, wrung from his very heart. Then he started slowly and laboriously, for his strength was fast failing, to swim to the boat.

By this time Hyla and Cerdic were in a safer position. The long-armed little man had made a great leap out of the water from Cerdic's shoulders. He pushed his friend far down beneath the surface with the force of his spring, but the slight resistance of Cerdic's body had given him the necessary impetus, and his strong arms clutched the keel. He was very soon astride it, and when Cerdic came spluttering up again he too was easily assisted into comparative safety.

Suddenly Huber saw the two seated there, and his white face became drawn and furrowed with despair as he saw his last hope gone.

"Hyla! Cerdic!" he called quaveringly, "ye two have beaten twelve brave men, and me among 'em. Ye have Godis grace with you, curse you! and I am done and over. Give you good-day."

"You fool, Huber!" said Hyla in concern, "think you we are foes in this pass? Wait, man, keep heart a little while!" He lifted his leg from the other side of the keel and dived into the water, sending the boat rocking away for yards as he did so. He made the exhausted archer place two hands upon his shoulders, and in ten exhausting minutes the three were perched upon the boat keel, the sole survivors of that ill-fated crew. The sun began to be hot, and they saw they were near land by now.

"I will just make a prayer," said Cerdic, with some apology. "It will do no harm, and perhaps please Our Lady, who, I wist, has done this for Hyla and me and Huber."

With that he fell fervently to uncouth thanksgivings, while the sun came rushing up and dried them all.

Hyla and Huber glanced at each other in mute admiration of his eloquence.

CHAPTER XII

"Through the gray willows danced the fretful gnat,
The grasshopper chirped idly from the tree,
 In sleek and oily coat the water-rat,
Breasting the little ripples manfully
Made for the wild-duck's nest."

They won to land, with the aid of a floating oar. Hyla and Cerdic were for getting back to Icomb and explaining what had befallen them to the fathers, but Huber flatly refused to accompany them. He said it was his duty to go back to Hilgay and say what had become of his comrades, and how they had met their end.

"But if you tell Lord Fulke how you have eaten and slept in friendship—for we must rest and eat before we go—with those that did kill his father, what then?" said Cerdic.

"Lord Fulke would not dare harm me for that, even were I to tell him. I am too well liked among the men. Natheless, I shall say nothing. I shall say that I clomb on the boat, and won the shore, and so made my way home. Look you to this. Can I give up the only life I know, and my master, and eke my wife to serve the priests, or live hunted and outlaw in the fens with you?" He argued it out with perfect fairness and good sense, and, with a sinking of the heart, they saw that their ways must indeed lie very far apart.

Material considerations made the whole thing difficult. They were in an unenviable position, and one of great danger, and their only means of transport was the one boat. "There is only one way," said Cerdic, "and that is this: we must row over the lake to the Priory first, and then leave the boat with Huber to make his own way back over the lake and through the fenways."

The man-at-arms crossed himself with fervour.

"Not I," he said. "I would not venture again upon that accursed lake for my life. It is cursed. You have heard of the Great Black Hand? It is an evil place, and has taken many of my good comrades. Leave you me here and go your ways. I will try to get back through the fen."

"Art no fenman, Huber, and canst scarcely swim. Also, that is the most dangerous part of the fen, the miles between the river and this lake. It's nought but pools, water-ways, and bog. You could not go a mile."

"Then I will stay here and rot. There is no mortal power that shall make me upon that water more."

There was such genuine superstitious terror in his face and voice that they felt it useless to attempt persuasion, and they cast about in their minds for some other solution of the difficulty. It was long in coming, for in truth the problem was very difficult. At last it was solved, poorly enough, but with a certain possibility of safety.

The three men had landed but a few hundred yards from the opening of the water-way which led to Hilgay, winding in devious routes among the fen. To regain the monastery there were two ways—One, the obvious route, by simply crossing the great lake, for the Abbey was almost exactly opposite, and the other, most difficult and dangerous, to skirt the lake side, where there was but little firm ground, and go right round it to the Priory.

Seeing no help for it, they decided on attempting that. Huber was to have the big, heavy boat, and as best he could, make his way back to Hilgay. It was a curious decision to have arrived at. By all possible rights, Hyla and Cerdic should have kept the boat for their own use, and let Huber shift as best he could. He was, or rather had been, an enemy; they had not only treated him with singular kindness, but he owed his very life to them. It is difficult to exactly gauge their motive. Probably their long slavery had something of its influence with them. Despite their new ideals and the stupendous upheaval of their lives, it is certain that they could hardly avoid regarding Huber from the standpoint of their serfdom. He had been one of their rulers, and there still clung to him some savour of authority. Yet it was not all this feeling that influenced them. Some nobler and deeper instinct of self-denial and kindness had made them do this thing.

In a closed locker, in the stern of the boat, they found some fishing lines, and a flint for making fire. It was easy to get food, and they spent the day resting and fishing. At length night fell softly over the wanderers, and they fell asleep round the fire, while the other went scraping among the reeds searching for fresh-water mussels, and the night wind sent black ripples over all the pools and the great lake beyond.

They were early up, catching more fish for breakfast, and, rather curiously for those times, they bathed in the fresh cold water, whereby they were most heartily refreshed and put into good courage. Then came the time of parting. It was fraught with a certain melancholy, for they had seemed very close together in their common danger.

"I doubt we shall ever clap eyes on you again, Huber," Hyla said. "Cerdic and I are not likely to trouble Hilgay again, unless indeed my lord catch us again, and I think there is but little fear of that."

"No, friend Hyla," said the man-at-arms; "we must say a long good-bye this morn."

"You will get back in a day," said Cerdic, "though boat be heavy and the way not easy. What tale will you tell Lord Fulke?"

"Just truth, Cerdic, though indeed I shall not tell all the truth. I shall tell how my good comrades died, and how I did win to land with you two, and left you by the mere. I shall tell Lord Fulke that I could not overcome you, for that you were two to my one, and eke armed. That you saved me from the water I must not say, though well I should like to do so. They would think that I was in league with you, and had failed in my duty, if I said anything to your credit."

"Without doubt," said Hyla.

"You are right, Huber. But I do not look to see Hilgay again."

"And I pray that you never may, friend, for your end would be a very terrible and bloody one. And now hear me. You have taken me to your hearts that did come to use you shamefully. My life is your gift, and I will save pennies that prayer may be made for you by some priest that you be kept from harm, and win quiet and safety. Moreover, never will I do ill to any serf again, for your sakes. For you are good and true men, and have my love. Often I shall remember you and the lake and all that has come about, when I am far away. And give me your hand and say farewell, and Lord Christ have you safe."

They said the saddest of all human words, "farewell," and turning he left them. The big boat moved slowly away among the reeds until it was hidden from their sight. Once they thought they heard his voice in a distant shout of farewell, and they called loudly in answer, but there was no response but the lapping of the water on the reeds.

"A true man," said Hyla sadly.

"I think so," said Cerdic, "and there are many like him also. We have never known them, or they us, but chance has changed that for once. Nevertheless I am not sorry he has gone. We are of one kind and he of another, and best apart. Let us set out round the lake; we have a long task before us, and I fear dangerous."

They gathered up their fishing lines and the remaining fish, which they had cooked for their journey, and set out upon it.

They were full of hope and courage, resolute to surmount the perils and difficulties which were before them, and yet, all innocent of fate, one was going to a sudden death and the other was moving towards an adventure which would end in death and torture also.

It is surely a very good and wise ordering of affairs, that we do not often have a warning of what shall shortly befall us. Only rarely do we feel the cold air from the wings of Death beat upon our doomed faces. Now and then, indeed, we get a glimpse of those unseen principalities and powers by whom we are for ever surrounded. Women in childbirth have, so it is said, seen an angel bearing them the new soul they are going to give to the world, as God's messenger came to Our Lady of old time.

More often the black angel, who is to take us from one life to another, presses upon a man's brain that he may know his near translation. Visions are given to men who have lived as men should live, and have beaten down Satan under their feet.

A wise and awful hand moves the curtain aside for them. And it is sometimes so with a great sinner. When that arch scoundrel Geoffroi was close upon his end, he also had a solemn warning. Fear came to him in the night and whispered, as you have heard, that he was doomed.

But these two children were given no sign. It was not for them; they could not have understood it. God is a psychologist, and He watched these two simple ones very tenderly.

A mile of heavy going lay behind them. Over the quaking fen bright with evil-looking flowers, as beautiful and treacherous as some pale sensual woman of the East, they plodded their weary and complacent way.

Lean, brown, old Cerdic was to die. Radiance was waiting for this poor man, as the sun—how dull beside that greater radiance which was so soon to illuminate him!—clomb up the sky.

They crossed various ditches and water-ways, leaping some and wading breast-high through others, covered with floating scum and weeds. Once or twice a wide pool of black water alive with fish brought them to a check, and they had to swim over it or make a long detour. After about three hours their journey became more easy. There was not so much water about, and the ground, which was covered with fresh, vividly green grass in wide patches, was much firmer.

Cerdic went on in front with a willow-pole, probing the ground to see if it was safe for them to venture on, a most necessary precaution in that land of bog and morass.

They were passing a clump of reeds when, with a quick scurry, a large hare ran out almost under their feet. Something had happened to one of its fore-legs, for it limped badly, and scrambled along at no great rate.

A hare's leg is a wonderfully fragile piece of mechanism, despite its enormous power. Often when the animal is leaping it over-balances itself in mid air, and coming down heavily breaks the thin bone. This is what had happened to the creature that startled them from the reeds.

The Serf

The quick eye of the old lawer-of-dogs saw at once that the animal was injured and could not go very fast. Here was a chance of food which would be very welcome. With a shout to Hyla he went leaping after it. His lean, brown legs spread over the ground, hardly seeming to touch it as he ran. He soon came up with the hare, but just as he was stooping to grasp it the creature doubled, and was off in a new direction. Hyla saw Cerdic pick himself up, stumble, recover, and flash away on the new track. In a minute a tall hedge of reeds, which seemed as if they might fringe a pool, hid him from view.

Hyla plodded slowly on, wondering if Cerdic would catch the hare, and thinking with a pleasant stomachic anticipation what a very excellent meal they might have if that were so. In about five minutes he came up to the reeds, and just as he approached them his heart gave a great leap of fear. Cerdic was calling him, but in a voice such as he had never heard him use before, it was so changed and terrible. Half shout, half whine, and wholly unnerving. He plunged through the cover, the wet splashing up round his feet in little jets as he did so, and then he came across his friend.

Six or more yards away there was a stretch of what at first glance appeared to be pleasant meadow land, so bright was the grass and so studded with flowers. In the centre of the space, which might measure twenty square yards, Cerdic stood engulfed to the waist, and rapidly sinking deeper. He made superhuman efforts to extricate himself. His arms beat upon the sward, and his hands clutched terribly at the tufts of grass and marsh flowers. His face, under all its tan, became a dark purple, as the terrible pressure on his body increased, and he began to bleed violently from the nose, and to vomit. Hyla went cautiously towards him, but every step he took became more dangerous, and he was forced to stand still in an agony of helplessness. Even in his own comparative security he could feel the soft caressing ground sucking eagerly at his feet.

He watched in horror. Slowly now, though with horrible distinctness, the body of his friend was going from him. The green grass lay round his arm-pits, and his arms were extended upon it at right angles like the arms of a man crucified. His fingers kept jumping up and down as if he were playing upon some instrument.

Then there came a gleam of hope. The motion ceased, and the head and upper part of the shoulders remained motionless.

"Have you touched bottom, Cerdic?" Hyla called in a queer high-pitched voice that startled himself.

"No, Hyla," came in thick, difficult reply, "and I die. I am going away from you, and must say farewell. I have loved you very well, and now good-bye. I am not afraid. Good-bye. I will pray to God as I die. Do you also pray, and farewell, farewell!"

He closed his staring eyes, and very gradually the sucking motion recommenced.

Hyla stared stupidly at this slow torture, unable to move or think.

It was soon over now, and the body sank very quickly away, and left the survivor gazing without thought at the spot where nothing marked a grave.

As he watched, a hare with a broken leg began to hobble across the vivid greenness.

CHAPTER XIII

"A most composed invincible man, in difficulty and distress knowing no discouragement, in danger and menace laughing at the whisper of fear."

There is a wonderful steadfast courage about men of Hyla's breed. Even though the object they pursue has lost its value, they go on in a dogged relentless "following up" from which nothing can turn them.

The Serf

For two hours or more he mourned and thought of old times, gazing in a kind of strange wonder at the silent carpet of grass. The shrewd weatherworn face, the twinkling eager eyes, the nasal drawl which so glibly offered up petitions to heaven, all came back to him with a singular vividness. He was surprised to find how actual and clear his friend's personality was to him. It almost frightened him. He glanced round him once or twice uneasily. Cerdic seemed so real and near, an unseen partner in the silence.

When one has heard bells tolling for a long time, and suddenly they stop, the brain is still conscious of the regular lin-lan-lone.

While this psychic influence eddied round him, and the kindly old face, ploughed deep with toil and sorrow, was still a veritable possession of his brain, there was a certain comfort.

As it began to fade, as day from the sky, his loneliness came upon him like death. The real agony of his loss began, and it tortured him until he could feel no more. Pain is its own anodyne in the end.

The cordage of his brave heart was so racked and strained by all he had endured that its capacity for sensation was over. So he mourned Cerdic dead no longer, his heart was dead.

But we know nothing of this poor brother, if not that in him was a sound piece of manhood, hardened, tempered, and strong. His soul was sweet and healthy, his rough-built body proud of blood and powerful. He must go on and fear nothing. Once more he must rise from his fall and try fortune with a stout sad heart, proving his own Godhead and the glory of his will, over which Fate could have no lordship.

In this only, as the poet sang, are men akin to gods, and in all life there is no glory like the "glory of going on."

Then did Hyla, the invincible, rise from the ground to breast circumstance—*per varios casus*—to seek his Latium once more.

He fell to eating cold roast fish.

When he set out again, he had to make a long detour. The sounding pole still remained to him, and he probed every step as he slowly skirted the treacherous green. It was characteristic of him that as he left the fatal spot where the dead Cerdic lay deep down in the mud he never looked round or gazed sadly at the place. He had no thought of sentimental leave-taking, no little poetic luxury of grief moved him. It were an action for a slighter brain than this.

It began to be late afternoon, as Hyla made a slow and difficult progress. He had got round the swamp, and pushed on over the fen. Sometimes he waded through stagnant pools fringed with rushes and covered with brilliant copper-coloured water plants. Once, pushing his pole before him, he swam over a wide black pond in which the sun was mirrored all blood red. Often he broke his way through forests of reeds which spiked up far above his head. Everywhere before him the creatures of the fen ran trembling.

Sometimes the firmer ground he came to was as brilliant as old carpets from the house of an Eastern king. The yellow broom moss was maturing, and bright chestnut-coloured capsules curved among it. The wild thyme crisped under his feet. The fairy down of the cotton grass floated round them.

Little tufts of pale sea-lavender nestled among the long leaves of the marsh zostera, plump, rank, and full of moisture. The fox-tail grass and the cat's-tail grass flourished everywhere.

We of to-day can have but a faint idea of that wonderful and luxuriant carpet over which he trod. The fair yellow corn now stands straight and tall over those solitudes. The

The Serf

broad dyke cut deep in the brown peat now straightly cleaves the fen, still beautiful and rich in life, but changed for ever from its ancient magic.

By night the lone sprites of the marsh with their ghostly lamps flit disconsolate, for the hand of man has come and tamed that teeming wilderness which was once so strange and alien from Man. Man was not wanted there in those old days, and the cruel swamps claimed a life-sacrifice as the price of their invasion.

Hyla's hard brown feet were all stained by the living carpet on which they walked. His advancing tread broke down the great vivid crimson balls of the *agaricus fungus*, and split its fat milk-white stem into creamy flakes. The crimson poison painted his instep, and the bright orange chanterelle mingled its harmless juice with that of its deadly cousin. His ankles were powdered with the dull pink-white of the hydnum, that strong mushroom on which they say the hedgehog feeds greedily at midnight, the tiny fruit of the "witches' butter" crumbled at his touch.

Over all, the fierce dragon-fly swung its mailed body, the Geoffroi of the fen insects.

The light and shadow sweeping over the wheat in its ordered planting are beautiful, but Hyla saw what we can never see in England more, saw with his steadfast, regardless eyes more natural beauties than we can ever see again.

In every clump of reeds that fringed the pool, he came suddenly upon some old pike basking in the sun, like a mitred bishop in his green and gold. The green water flags trembled as he sunk away.

The herons paddled in the shallow pools, and tossed the little silver fish from them to each other, the cold-eyed hawk dropped like a shooting star, and fought the stoat for his new-killed prey.

The shadows lengthened and lay in patches over the wild world of water. The blue mists began to rise from a hundred pools, and the bats to flicker through them. The sunlight faded rapidly away, the world became greyish ochre colour, then grey, a soft cobweb grey, through which fell the hooting of an owl, and the last call of a plover.

Resolute, though wearied and faint, firm in resolve, though with a bitter loneliness at his heart, Hyla plunged on through the twilight. For some little time the ground had been much firmer and a little raised above the level of the fen, but as day was dying, he found he had entered upon a long and gradual slope, and that once more it behoved him to walk with infinite care.

Old rotting tree-trunks cropped up here and there, relics of some vast, ancient forest, which, mingling with rotting vegetation of all kinds, sent up a smell of decay in his nostrils. At every step he sank up to the knees, and brown water, the colour of brandy, splashed up to his waist.

He seemed to have arrived at a more desolate evil part of the fens than before. The approaching night made his progress more and more difficult. It was here that the night herons had their nests and breeding-places, inaccessible to men. The ground was bespattered with their excrements, and with feathers, broken egg-shells, old nests, and half-eaten fish covered with yellow flies.

Then as he ploughed on he saw a sight at which even his stout heart failed him. His long struggle seemed suddenly all in vain. Right before him was a wide creek or arm of the lake, two hundred yards from reeds to reedy shore, entirely barring the way. Too far for him to swim, all dead-weary as he was, mysterious and ugly in the faint light, it gave him over utterly to despair.

It began to be cold, and the chilly marsh-vapour crept into his bones and turned the marrow of them to ice.

He sat on a mound formed by a great log and the *dèbris* of a mass of decayed roots, the whole damp and cold as a fish's belly, and covered with living fungi and slimy moss. His feet were buried in the brown water.

It was now too dark to move in any direction with safety, and until day should break again he must remain where he was. He had no more food of any kind, and was absolutely exhausted. So he moaned a little prayer, more from habit than from any comfort in the act, and stretching himself over the damp moss fell into a fitful sleep. He dreamed he was back at the Priory, and heard in his dreaming the distant sound of the monks singing prayers.

It was a picture of his own life, this sorry end to all his day's endeavour. It foreshadowed his career, so rapidly darkening down into death. His life-path, trod with such bitterness, growing ever more devious and painful, while the *ignes fatui* of Hope danced round its closing miles!

CHAPTER XIV

"So, some time, when the last of all our evenings
Crowneth memorially the last of all our days,
Not loth to take his poppies, man goes down and says:
'*Sufficient for the day were the day's evil things.*'"

Free will, warring with fate, produces Tragedy, so it is said. To-day, we have lost much of the significance of the old "τραγωίδα." When the priest poets Tyrtæus and Æschylus clamorously exalted—held high that all might see—the Godhead of men who fight and do, it was not so much the tragedy itself, but the circumstances that made it which inspired men's hearts.

"Free will warring with Fate"—it was the clash of that fine battle, which those old Greeks found significant and uplifting.

For a moment let us look into this so seeming-piteous a one of ours, on which soon the iron curtain is resonantly to fall.

It is a hard, stern story this of our poor serf. The rebel lifted his hand against an established force. For that he perished in bitter agony. But, going so soon to his death, he shows us a Man in spite of all his woes. And we can be uplifted in contemplating that. It is Hyla's message to us no less than to his scarred brethren on the castle hill.

The Lord of Hilgay could maim and kill his body, but the Manhood in him was a flame unquenchable, and burnt a mark upon his age. The clash of his battle rings through centuries.

His doings sowed a seed, and we ourselves sit to-day in that great blood-nourished tree of Freedom which sprang therefrom.

The stars that night were singularly bright and vivid. The sky was powdered with a dust of light, among which the greater stars burned like lamps.

Below that glorious canopy Hyla lay in an uneasy sleep. Every now and then he awoke, chilled to the bone. Though the stars were all so clear and bright they seemed very remote from this world and all its business, as he looked up with staring, miserable eyes. Hyla believed, as little children in Spain are taught to this day, that the stars were but chinks, holes, and gaps in the floor of heaven itself. He thought their bright white light but an overflow of the great white radiance of God's Home.

That comforted him but little as he lay cold and hungry in the swamp. Indeed it was easier to pray in the day-time, when even a hint of heaven was absent. The enormous radiance was so remote in its splendour. It accentuated his forlorn and forgotten state.

He was lying but a few yards from the edge of the broad pool which barred his progress, and as the hours wore on and the stars paled, the blackness of the water became grey and tremulous.

It was nearing dawn, though the sun had not yet risen, when he thought he saw a red flicker in the mist which lay over the lagoon. It was too ruddy and full-coloured for a marsh light, and his hopes leapt up, half doubting, at the sight. In a moment or two, the light became plainer, and he knew he was not deceived. The thing was real. It advanced towards him, and seemed like a torch.

He sent a husky shout out over the water. Whether the light betokened advance of friend or foe he did not know or care.

No answer came to his call, but he saw the red light become stationary immediately, and cease to flicker.

He shouted again louder than before, standing up on the rotting log, and filling his lungs with air. An answering voice came out of the mist at this, and the light moved again.

And now the grey waste began to tremble with light. The sun was rising, and at the first hint of his approach, the mists began to sway and dissolve.

Coming straight towards the bank, Hyla saw a fen punt urged by a tall, thin man dressed in skins like a serf. He used the long pole with skill, and seemed thoroughly at home in the management of his boat.

About six yards from the shore, he dug his pole deep down and checked the motion of the punt. Hyla waded down among the mud as far as was safe, and hailed him. "For the love of God, sir," he said, "take me from this swamp."

The stranger regarded him fixedly for a moment, without answering. Then he spoke in a slow, deliberate, but resonant voice.

"Who are you? How have you come here in this waste? I thought no man could come where you are."

"I am starving for food," said Hyla, "and like to die in the marsh an you do not take me in your boat. I am of Icomb, thrall to the Prior Sir Richard. The Lord of Hilgay's men took me and another who lies dead in the swamp. They were upon the big lake when the boat upset, and all were drowned save one. He has got him back to the castle, and I am journeying to Icomb, if perchance I may come there safely."

"You tell of strange things," said the tall man, "and I will presently ask you more of them. Now hearken. I am not one of those who give, taking nothing in return. I will take you safe back to the Fathers, and feed you with food. But for three days you must labour for me in work that waits to be done in my field. I need a man's arm."

"For a week. If by that you will save me from this."

"So be it," said the tall man with great promptness. "You shall work for a week, and then I will take you to Icomb."

With that he loosened the dripping pole, drove it again into the water, and the nose of the punt glided up to Hyla.

He clambered carefully on board, and sat dripping.

"I have no food here," said the man, "for I live hard by, and did but come out to look at some lines I set down overnight, but we shall soon be there."

As he spoke he was poling vigorously, and they were already half way over the pool.

The Serf

As they neared the opposite shore, Hyla saw the reeds grew to a great height above them, forming a thick screen with apparently an unbroken face. But he knew that suddenly they would come upon an opening which would be quite imperceptible to the ordinary eye, and so it proved.

With a sure hand the stranger sent the bows at a break but a yard wide in the reeds. The punt went hissing through the narrow passage, pushing the reeds aside for a moment, only that they should spring back again after its passage. A few yards through the thick growth brought them into a circular pool or basin. This also was surrounded with reeds which towered up into the air. It was very small in diameter, and floating on its placid black water was like being at the bottom of a jar.

The place was full of the earliest sunlights and busy with the newly awakened life of the fen.

But what arrested the serf's immediate attention was a curious structure at the far side of the pool. It resembled nothing so much as a small house-boat. A wooden hut had been built upon a floating platform of timber, and the whole was moored to a stout pile which projected some three feet from the water.

A fire smouldered on the deck in front of the hut, and a cooking pot hung over it by a chain.

"This is my home," said the man, pointing towards the raft. "Where I go I take my house with me, and ask no man's leave. I have lived on this pool for near two years now."

They landed on the raft.

"Now you shall fill your belly, Sir Wanderer," said the man, "and then I will hear more of you. Here is a mess of hare, marsh quail, and herbs. It's fit for a lord eke a thrall, for I see you wear a thrall's collar. Here is a wooden bowl, fill it, and so thyself."

He came out of the cabin with two rough wooden bowls, which he dipped and filled in the cauldron.

Then for a space, while the sun rode up the sky, there was no sound heard but the feeding of hungry men.

Hyla began to feel the blood moving in him once more, and the strength of manhood returning. The sun shone on his chilled limbs and warmed them, the night was over.

At the finish of the meal the tall man turned on him suddenly and without preparation. "How should Hyla of the long arms, thrall of Geoffroi de la Bourne, be making his way to Richard Espec? Has the devil then made friends with Holy Church? Is Geoffroi about to profess for a monk?"

Hyla stared at him stupidly with open mouth, and swift fear began to knock at his heart.

"I doubt me there is something strange here," said the tall man, with a sudden bark of anger. "There is something black here, my good rogue. I pray you throw a little light upon this. If ever I saw a man with fear writ upon him you are that man, Hyla. I beg leave to think there are others of you not far away! There are more from Hilgay about us in the fen."

Hyla glanced hurriedly round the quiet little pool. "Where? where?" he said in a tone of unmistakable terror. "Have you seen them, then? Are they in wait to take me?"

The other looked at him with a long searching glance for near a minute.

"We two be at a tangle," he said at length. "You are in flight, then, from the Hilgay men?"

"For my life," said Hyla.

The Serf

"Then you and I are in one boat, Hyla, as it is said. I doubted that you had come against me just now. So they are after you? Have you been killing game in the forest or stealing corn?"

"It was game," said Hyla quickly; "big game," he added in an uneasy afterward.

There was silence for a minute. The long, lean man seemed turning over something in his mind.

"So you got to Icomb for sanctuary," he said slowly. "And Geoffroi sent his men after you. It is a long way through the fen to go after one thrall. And also they say Lord Roger Bigot is going to Hilgay with a great host. It is unlike Geoffroi de la Bourne to waste men hunting for a serf at such a time. He is growing old and foolish."

Hyla glanced at him quickly. He knew by the man's mocking tone that he was disbelieved. Hyla was but a poor liar.

"Then you know Lord Geoffroi?" he said, stumbling woefully over the words.

"I know him," said the man slowly. "I am well acquainted with that lord, though it is eight years since we have met." Suddenly his voice rose, though he seemed to be trying to control it. "God curse him!" he cried in a hoarse scream; "will the devil never go to his own place!"

Hyla started eagerly. The man's passion was so extreme, his curse was so real and full of bitter hatred that an avowal trembled on his lips.

The other gave him the cue for it.

"Come, man," he said briskly, resuming his ordinary voice; "you are keeping something. Tell out straight to one who knows you and Gruach also—does that surprise you? There are no friends of the house of Bourne here. What is it, what hast done?"

"Killed him," said Hyla shortly.

"Splendeur dex!" said the man in a fierce whisper. His face worked, his eyes became prominent, he trembled all over with excitement, like a hunting dog scenting a quarry while in the leash.

Then he burst out into a torrent of questions in French, the foreign words tumbling over each other in his eagerness.

Hyla knew nothing of what he said, for he had no French. Seeing his look of astonishment, the man recovered himself. "I forgot for a moment," he said, "who you were. Now thank God for this news! So, you have killed him! At last! At last! How and why? Say quickly."

Hyla told him in a few words all the story.

"And who are you, then?" he said, when he had done.

"I call myself Lisolè to the few that I meet in the fen. But agone I had another name. Come and see."

He took Hyla by the arm and led him into the cabin. It was a comfortable little shelter. A couch of skins ran down one side, and above it were shelves covered with pots, pans, tools, and fishing gear. A long yew-bow stood in one corner among a few spears. An arbalist lay upon a wooden chest. Light came into the place through a window covered with oiled sheep-skin stretched upon a sliding frame. In one corner was an iron fire-pan for use in winter, and a hollow shaft of wood above it went through the roof in a kind of chimney.

The place was a palace to Hyla's notions. No serf had such a home. The cabin was crowded with possessions. Unconsciously Hyla began to speak with deference to this owner of so much.

"See here," said the man. At the end of the cabin was a broad shelf painted in red, with a touch of gilding. A thick candle of fat with a small wick, which gave a tiny glimmer of light, was burning in an iron stand. In the wall behind, was a little doorless cupboard, or alcove, in which was a small box of dark wood, heavily bound round with iron bands. At the back of the alcove a cap of parti-coloured red and yellow was nailed to the wall.

The man who called himself Lisolè lifted the box from the alcove carefully, and as he did so the edge touched a bell on the end of the pointed cap. It tinkled musically.

Hyla crossed himself, for the place he saw was a shrine, and the iron-bound coffer held the relic of some saint.

"On this day," said the man, "I will show you what no other eyes than mine have seen for eight long, lonely years. I doubt nothing but that it is God His guidance that has brought you here to this place. For to you more than all other men this sight is due."

So saying, he fumbled in his coat, and pulled therefrom a key, which hung round his neck upon a cord of twisted gut.

He opened the box and drew several objects from it. One was a great lock of nut-brown hair, full three feet long, as soft and fine as spun silk. Another was a ring of gold, in which a red stone shone darkly in the candle-light. There were one or two pieces of embroidered work, half the design being uncompleted, and there was a Christ of silver on a cross of dark wood.

"They were Isoult's," said the man in a hushed voice.

"Isoult la Guèrisseur?" said Hyla.

"Isoult, the Healer."

"Then you who are called Lisolè——?"

"Was once Lerailleur, whose jesting died eight years ago. It was buried in Her grave."

"God and Our Lady give her peace," said Hyla, crossing himself. "See you this scar on my arm? A shaft went through it in the big wood. Henry Montdefeu was hunting with Lord Geoffroi. I was beating in the undergrowth, and a chance shaft came my way. La Guèrisseur bound it up with a mess of hot crushed leaves and a linen strip. In a week I was whole. That was near ten years ago."

"You knew me not?"

"Nor ever should have known hadst not told me. Your hair it is as white as snow, your face has fallen in and full of lines, aye, and your voice is not the voice that sang in the hall in those days."

"Ah, now I am Lisolè. But thank God for this day. I can wait the end quiet now. So you have killed him! Know you that I also tried? I was not bold as you have been. I tried with poison, and then fled away by night. I took the poppy seeds—*les pavois*—and brewed them, and put the juice in his drink. But I heard of him not long after as well and strong, so I knew it was not to be. I never knew how I failed."

"I can tell you that," said Hyla, "it was common talk. Lord Geoffroi went to his chamber in Outfangthef Tower drunken after dinner in the hall. Dom Anselm led him there, and the priest was sober that night, or 'twould have been Geoffroi's last. On the table was his night-draught of morat in which you had put the poison. Geoffroi drank a long pull, and then fell on the bed and lay sleeping heavy among the straw. Dom Anselm, being thirsty, did go to take a pull at the morat, but scarce put lip to it when the taste or smell told him what it was. Hast been a chirurgeon, they do say, and knoweth simples as I the fen-lands. So he ran for oil and salt, and poureth them into Geoffroi until he vomited the poison. But for two days after that he was deadly sick and could hold no food. I mind well they searched the forest lands for you and eke the fen, but found not."

"Aye, I fled too swiftly and too far for such as they. It takes wit to be a fool, and they being not fools but men-at-arms had no cunning such as mine. I built this house of mine with wood from Icomb, and have lived upon the waters this many a year."

"Ever alone and without speech of men?"

"Not so. Sometimes I get me to Mass at Icomb, and I am well with the monks. And sometimes they bring a sick brother to this place to touch this hair and cross, and be cured. For know, Hyla, that my wife, a healer in her life, still heals by favour of Saint Mary, being gone from this sad world and with Lord Christ in heaven. The Fathers would have me bring these relics to Icomb there to be enshrined, and I to profess myself a monk. Often have they sent messengers to persuade me. But I would not go while He was living, for I could not live God's life hating him so. But now perchance I shall go. It will bear thinking of."

They knelt down before the lock of hair and the crucifix and prayed silently.

It was a strange meeting. This man Lerailleur had been buffoon to Geoffroi, and had come with him from Normandy. His wife, Isoult, was a sweet simple dame, so fragrant and so pure that all the world loved her. She was a strangely successful nurse and doctor, and knew much of herbs. In those simple times her cures were thought miraculous, and she was venerated. The jester, a grave and melancholy man when not professionally employed, thought her a saint, and loved her dearly. Now one winter night, Lord Geoffroi being, as was his wont, very drunk, set out from his feasting in the hall to seek sleep in his bed-chamber.

Isoult had been watching by the side of a woman—wife to one of the men-at-arms—who was brought to bed in child-birth. She crossed the courtyard to her own apartment, in front of Geoffroi de la Bourne. He, being mad with drink, thought he saw some phantom, and drew his dagger. With a shout he rushed upon the lady, and soon she lay bleeding her sweet life away upon the frosty ground.

They buried her with great pomp and few dry eyes, and Geoffroi paid for many Masses, while Lerailleur bided his time. The rest we have heard.

Hyla and Lisolè sat gravely together on the deck of the boat. The relics were put away in their shrine.

Neither said much for several hours, the thoughts of both were grave and sad, and yet not wholly without comfort.

They seemed to see God's hand in all this. There was something fearful and yet sweet in their hearts. So Sintram felt when he had ridden through the weird valley and heard Rolf singing psalms.

The "midsummer hum"—in Norfolk they call the monotone of summer insect life by that name—lulled and soothed them. There was peace in that deep and secret hiding-place.

In the afternoon they broiled some firm white fish and made another meal. "Come and see my field," said Lisolè afterwards.

They got into the small punt and followed a narrow way through the reeds, going away from the wide stretch of water on the further shore of which they had first met. At a shelving turfy shore they disembarked.

Climbing up a bank they came suddenly upon three acres of ripening corn, a strange and pastoral sight in that wilderness. Small dykes covered with bright water-flowers ran through the field dividing it into small squares. It was thoroughly drained, and a rich crop.

"All my own work, Hyla," said the ex-jester, with no inconsiderable pride in his voice. "I delved the ditches and got all the water out of the land. Then I burnt dried reeds over it, and mixed the ashes with the soil for a manure. Then I sowed my wheat, and it is bread, white bread, all the year round for me. I flail and winnow, grind and bake, and no man helps me. The monks would lend me a thrall to help, but I said no. I am happier alone, La Guèrisseur seems nearer then. I have other things to show you, but not here. Let us go back to home first. To-day is a holiday, and you also need rest."

When the moon rose and the big fishes were leaping out of the water with resonant echoing splashes in the dusk, they were still sitting on the deck of the boat in calm contemplation.

They spoke but little, revolving memories. Now and then the jester made some remark reminiscent of old dead days, and Hyla capped it with another.

About ten o'clock, or perhaps a little later, a long, low whistle came over the water to them, in waves of tremulous sound. Lisolè jumped up and loosened the painter of the punt. "It's one of the monks," he said; "now and again they come to me at night time."

Hyla waited as the punt shot off into the alternation of silver light and velvet shadow. Before long he heard voices coming near, and the splash of the pole. It was a monk from Icomb, a ruddy, black-eyed, thick-set man. His coracle was towed behind the punt.

He greeted the serf with a "benedicite," and told him that Lisolè had given him the outlines of his story.

"Anon, my son," said he, "you shall go back with me to peace. We thought, indeed, that you had left us with the thrall Cerdic, and we were not pleased. Your wife and daughter have been in a rare way, so they tell me."

For long hours, as Hyla fell asleep covered with a skin upon the deck, he heard the low voices of the monk and his host in the cabin. It was a soothing monotone in the night silence.

In the morning Lisolè came to him and woke him. "The father and I have talked the night through," he said, "and soon I leave my home for Icomb. 'Twill be better so. We will start anon. It is hard parting, even with this small dwelling, but it is Godys will, I do not doubt."

CHAPTER XV

"Though you be in a place of safety, do not, on that account, think yourself secure."—Saint Bernard.

Brother Felix, the monk who had come to them from Icomb, bade them rest another day before setting out over the lake.

"Ye have had a shrewd shog, Lisolè, in the news that Hyla brought, and he also has gone hardly of late. Let us rest a day and eat well, and talk withal. There is a bottle of clary that the Prior sent. It is good to rest here."

His merry black eyes regarded them with an eminent satisfaction at his proposal. It was his holiday, this trip from the Priory, and he had no mind to curtail it.

There was yet a quaint strain of melancholy humour about the ex-fool. The joy had gone, the wit lingered. His sojourn alone among the waters had mellowed it, added a new virtue to the essential sadness of the jester.

And Felix was no ordinary man. He had been an epicure in such things once. What the time could give of culture was his. He had been a writer of MS., a lay scriptor in the house of the Bishop at Rouen; he had illuminated missals in London, was a good Latinist, and, even in that time, had a little Greek. A day with Lisolè was a most pleasant variant to a life which he lived with real endeavour, but which was sometimes at war with his mental needs.

So they sat out on deck, among all the medley of the jester's rough household goods, on deck in the sunshine, while the monk and the prospective novice ranged over their experiences.

Hyla had never heard such talk before. Indeed, it is not too much to say that through all the years of his life he had never, until this day, been present at a *conversation*. Nearly all the words the serf had heard, almost all the words he himself had spoken, were about things which people could touch and see.

He and his friends, Cerdic notably, had touched on the unseen things of religion— "principalities and powers" who dominated the future—in their own uncouth way. But conversation about the abstract things of this earthly life he had rarely heard before.

For the first hour the novelty of it almost stunned him. He listened without thought, drinking it all in with an eagerness which defied consideration. It was his first and last social experience!

"Wilt not be so lonely in the cloister, friend," said Felix.

"Say you so?" answered the jester. "Yet to be alone is a powerful good thing. I have but hardly felt lack of humans this many a year. Many sorry poor ghosts of friends, gone to death back-along, come to me at night-time."

"And she, that saint that was thy wife, comes she to thee, Lisolè?"

"Betimes she comes, and ever with healing to my brain; but it is not the wife who slept by my side."

"More Saint and less Woman! Is that truth?"

Lisolè nodded sadly. The big monk stretched himself out at length so that the hot sun rays should fall on every part of him.

"I have no more to do with women," he said; "but in those other days I liked a woman to be a very woman, and not too good. Else, look you, wherein lieth the pleasure? It is because of the difference. Never cared I for a silent woman. If you would make a pair of good shoon, take the tongue of a woman for the sole thereof. It will not wear away. Full many a worthless girl has enslaved me—me whom no enemy ever did. Yet knowing all and seeing all, yet loved I all of them. And now—quantum mutatus ab illo!"

He sighed, a reminiscent sigh. "They took from me all I had," he continued, "and being poor and in distress I turned my thoughts Godwards."

"Women, priests, and pullets have never enough," said Lisolè with a sudden and quaint return of his professional manner. "They are past all understanding, save only the saints. Truly I have found a woman to be both apple and serpent in one. A woman, she is like to a fair table spread with goodly meats that one sees with different eyes before and after the feast."

"But hast feasted, brother, natheless? Forget not that."

"Art right, and it was well said. One should take bitter and sweet together. Yet, friend, I do not doubt but that when the Lord Jesus fed the concourse out of His charity and miracle, there were some at that feast who told one another the bread was stale and the fish too long out o' water! Men are so made. It is so in this life."

"Aye, and thou doest well in leaving this world for the Church's peace. Now thy enemy is dead and thy hate with him thou shalt find peace, even as I have done. For in what a pass is England! Peace being altogether overthrown love is cooled; all the land is moist with weeping, and all friendship and quietness is disappeared. All seek consolation and quiet. Almost all the nobles spend their time in contriving evil; the mad esquires delight in malice. These cruel butchers despise doctrine, and the holy preachers have no effect.

These men will not be amended by force of sermons, nor do they take any account of the lives of men. They all plunder together like robbers."

His voice rose in indignation, and both Hyla and the jester raised their heads in bitter acquiescence.

It was so true of that dark time. Each one there was a waif of life, a somewhat piteous jetsam from the dark tides which had almost overwhelmed them. The Anglo-Norman song was very true—

"*Boidie ad seignurie, pes est mise suz pè.*"

("The fraud of the rulers prevails, peace is trodden underfoot.")

Lisolè began to sing the air under his breath. The monk stopped him. "Not so," he said. "I was wrong to speak of these things to-day. They have passed us by. And this is my holiday, and I would not have it a sad one withal. We have no cause for sadness, we three. Let us eat, for our better enjoyment. Sun hath clomb half-way upon his journey, and I am hungry."

He bustled about, helping them to prepare the meal.

"Wine, fish, and eke wheaten-cakes," he cried merrily. "Do not we read in the Gospels that it was Christ His fare?"

Hyla noticed that a curious change had taken place in his host's face. The strained, brooding look in his eyes had disappeared. Already it was calmer, happier.

The monk, full of meat and once more basking in the heat, began to chat on all trivial subjects. He made little, aimless, lazy jests; contentment was exhaled from him.

The sun seemed to draw out the latent humour on the jester's countenance. He capped one remark by another; on the eve of taking the Vows, the clown flickered up in him, as though to rattle the bells once more in a last farewell.

Felix had thrown off his habit, and his massive neck and chest, covered with black hair, lay open to the genial warmth. His black hair and eyes, his ruddy cheeks, were in fine colour contrast; he was a study in black and crimson. He lay at length, his head pillowed on a cat-skin rug, and looked up at Lisolè, who leaned his length against the side of the cabin.

The jester had a thin metal rod in his hand, part of his cooking apparatus, his poker in fact, and all unconsciously he began to use it to emphasise his remarks—the fools bâton of his happier days. Now that the pressure on his brain, the dead-weight of hate, had been removed, a kind of reflex action took place. He became a little like his former self.

"Old Fenward," said the monk, "thou art changing as the worm to the winged fly! Thy wit fattens and mars with sorrow! On this day of deliverance make some sport for us; show thy old tricks, as Seigneur David leapt before the Lord. There is no sin in mirth— out of cloister," he added with a sudden afterthought, as a quick vision of Richard Espec crossed his mind.

Hyla sat at the edge of the little deck and looked on, wondering, his hard brown feet just touched the water. His face had sunk once more into its old passive unemotional aspect. A gaudy marsh fly, in its livery of black and yellow, had settled upon his hand, but he made no movement to brush it away.

The trio were beautifully grouped against the background of vivid green reeds, surrounded by the still brown water. To any one coming suddenly upon the quaint old boat lying among the white and yellow water-flowers, and its strange distinctive crew, the picture would have remained for long as an unforgettable mental possession.

The accidents of time, place, and colour, had so beautifully blended into a perfectly proportioned whole that it seemed more of design than chance.

The Serf

Lisolè smiled down at the big man. "My jesting days are long gone by," he said. "But, messires, I will try my hand for you this noon if perchance it has not lost all cunning. Once I had knowledge of the art of legerdemain, by which the hands, moving very swiftly and with concealed motions, do so trick and deceive the eye that he knows not what a-hath seen."

With a gurgle of satisfaction, Brother Felix sat up and propped himself against the cabin. Hyla drew nearer, with attentive eyes.

Lisolè left them for a moment and went inside the cabin. He came out with several articles in his hands, which he put beside him on the deck.

He showed them his bare hands, and then suddenly stretching out his right arm he caught at the empty air, and, behold! there came into his hand, how they could not tell, a little rod of black wood a foot in length or more.

A swift change came into his voice. It sank a full tone and became very solemn. His face was very grave. Hyla watched him with wide eyes and parted lips.

He turned to the serf, "Now, Hyla," said he, "art about to witness art magic, but none of Satan's, so be brave. Take you this little wand of enchaunted ebon-wood and say what dost make of it."

Very timidly, and with a half withdrawal, Hyla's great brown paw took the toy. He examined it, smelt it like a dog, and then with some relief gave it back to the owner.

"'Tis but a little stick of wood," he said.

"Natheless, a stick of good magic, thrall, for 'twas of this wood that the coffin of Mahound was built."

Hyla crossed himself reverently. He was surprised to see the monk was smiling easily. "The holy man has known these things of old," thought he, with a humble recognition of his own limitations and ignorance. "He seemeth nothing accoyed."

Lisolè cleared a space on the deck in front of him, and laid the wand upon it. Then he stretched out his hand over it, as though in invocation. "*By the Garden of Alamoot where thou grew*," he cried, "*and by the virtue of the blood of Count Raymond of Tripoli, whose blood fell on thee as he died in that garden, I command thee to do my will, little black stick.*"

He took a little pipe of reed from his belt, and, stopping one end with his finger, blew softly through it.

A mellow flute-like note quivered through the air. Hardly pausing for breath, the jester continued the monotonous cooing sound for several minutes.

Hyla watched the wand with fascinated eyes. Suddenly it began to tremble slightly and to roll this way and that. The pipe changed its notes and broke into the lilt of a simple dance. Simultaneously with the change the little stick rose up on its end and inclined itself gravely to each of them in turn. Then it began to hop up and down, retreating and advancing, in time to the music.

Hyla's tongue clave to the roof of his mouth. His lips were hot and dry, his throat seemed as if he had been eating salt.

A horrid fear began to rise within him, such strange fear as he had never known, as he watched the devilish little stick—how human it was!—in its fantastic dance. He did not see that both Felix and Lisolè were regarding him with the most intense amusement. The monk was grinning from ear to ear, and his hands were pressed to his sides in the effort to control a paroxysm of internal laughter.

Suddenly the music stopped. The stick ceased all movement, standing upright upon its end. Then—horror!—very slowly, but with great deliberation, it began to hop towards

The Serf

Hyla. Nearer and nearer it came, in little jumps of an inch or so. The tan of the serf's face turned a dusky cream colour, he put out both hands to ward off the evil thing.

But it hopped on relentlessly.

It came within a foot or two, and Hyla's terror welled up within him so fiercely that he gave a loud cry, stepped back, and with an echoing splash disappeared into the water over the boat side.

He rose almost immediately, spluttering and gasping, the shock depriving him of his senses.

Peals of laughter, echoing uncontrollable peals, saluted him. Felix thundered out his joy, the jester's thin voice shrieked in merriment.

Hyla trod water, staring at them in amazement.

"Come aboard, man! Come aboard!" cried the monk at length. "'Twas naught but a jest, a jougleur's trick, oh slayer of Lords!" His laughter forbade speech once more.

They helped the poor fellow on deck once more, and reassured him. But it was long before he began to like his company again. He remembered the shrine inside the cabin, the sudden appearance of the jester's torch through the mists of night, and longed most devoutly to be back at work on the good brown fields.

Till evening fell and supper-time was at hand, Lisolè entertained them. Never had he been more skilful and more full of humour than on this, his "farewell appearance," as he would have called it nowadays.

In his hands a wild duck's egg came, went, and changed, until Hyla's arm was tired with crossing himself. Water poured into an earthen jar changed into chopped straw in a single moment. Never were such wonders before on earth.

But as day went, so gaiety went with it. And before rest the monk said prayers at the lighted shrine of Isoult the Healer. He prayed for a safe passage over the waters on the morrow, and that the healing virtues of the relics before them might grow stronger and more powerful as they reposed before the Host in Church.

Then they all said the Lord's Prayer together, and so to sleep.

But Hyla's rest was fitful and disturbed. Strange broken dreams flitted through it. Often during the night he lay awake and heard the heavy snoring of his companions. The sound brought little sense of companionship with it. He was alone with his thoughts and the night.

In the early morning they set forth gravely, as befitted the solemn business they were about.

The precious coffer was laid reverently upon a bed of reeds in the punt, and, as the air was very still, the thick candle was lighted and placed before it. It was a very feeble, dusty, yellow gleam in the sunshine.

They set slowly out, down the brown channel among the rushes. The birds were singing.

The monk blessed the boat and the holy relics, and Lisolè took a last long look at his floating home ere they turned a corner and it passed from view.

He was very silent now that he had left everything. His thoughts were sad, for he was but human. That little refuge had been Home. He had been alone with the memory of Isoult there. They forged up the creek towards the lake, and his eyes fell upon the iron-bound box.

Then his face brightened. He set it towards the Island of Icomb, and made the sign of the cross. Nor did he look back any more.

The Serf

About half-way over the lake they rested, and ate some bread and broiled fish. Till then Hyla's strong arms had rowed them, and now Lisolè prepared to relieve him.

They were busy with the victuals in the bottom of the boat when a shout floated over the water, sudden and startling. They had thought no one near.

Looking up they saw a large boat manned by many oars, but two hundred yards away. It was strange they had not heard the rattle in the rowlocks.

A man in a shirt of chain mail stood upright in the bows, and a levelled cross-bow threatened them.

They gazed stupidly at the advancing terror. In forty seconds the boat was lying motionless beside them. Hyla saw many cruel, exulting, well-known faces. The monk began Latin prayers. Lisolè grasped the iron-bound box.

Suddenly Hyla became aware that a harsh voice was speaking. "We have no quarrel with you, Sir Monk, nor with your boatman. Natheless, unless you wish death, you will give that serf Hyla up to us without trouble. We are in luck to-day. We but thought to find the bodies of dead friends."

The rapid pattering Latin went on unceasingly, Hyla was lifted from the punt by strong, eager arms. A push sent the smaller vessel gliding away, he saw the distance opening out between—the ripples sparkled in the sun.

The wail of a farewell floated towards him, and then some one struck him a heavy blow upon the head, and everything flashed away.

CHAPTER XVI

"In that same conflict (woe is me!) befell,

This fatall chaunce, this dolefull accident

Whose heavy tidings now I have to tell.

First all the captives which they here had hent

Were by them slaine by generall consent."

Dom Anselm was strolling about the courtyard of the castle at Hilgay.

His hands were behind his back, and his head was thrust forward and slowly oscillated from side to side.

It was about eleven o'clock in the morning, and he was pretending to take an intelligent interest in the activity all round. He regarded four great bundles of newly made arrows tied up with rope in the manner of a connoisseur. He even took one out from its bundle, felt the point, and held it on a level with his eye to make sure that the shaft was perfectly straight and true.

Then he went to a heap of raw hides and felt their texture. This done he stood before a mangonel, which was being hoisted up upon the walls by a windlass, and surveyed it with an affectation of the engineer and a flavour of the expert at home. But he did it very badly, and the whole proceeding was an obvious effort. After that, feeling that he had done his duty, he went to the draw-well in the centre of the courtyard, and, sitting on the ground on the shady side—for it was a structure of masonry some four feet high, like all Norman walls—composed himself to sleep. The creature felt out of place. Upon first news of the coming attack he was hard at work shriving blackguards, and allowing each one to believe that should an arrow of the enemy put a swift end to his sinful life, the saints and angels would meet them at the jasper gates of heaven with trumpets and acclamations. The fools believed him; it flattered them to hear of these fine things provided for an unpleasant contingency, and no one was more important than Sir Anselm.

The Serf

Then came the ceremonial importance of the funeral and the votive Mass. That kept him well in the public eye for a little time. But this and that done, he found time hang very heavy upon his hands.

All round him activity was being pushed to its furthest limit, and in all that hive he was the only drone. The squires passed him with a jest, the waiting maids threw a quip at him. Lewin alone was friendly, but the minter had but little time to spare. That quick brain and alert eye for the main chances in life were very valuable at Hilgay, and Lewin was in constant request. The man suggested, advised, and directed operations which were the wonder of all who saw them.

But he said nothing of the crack in the orchard wall.

The precious couple were quite resolved upon the treachery which they had plotted in the fen. In truth Fulke was a bestial young fool, and offered no inducement to his followers to be faithful. Roger Bigot was a bigger man in the world, and reputed to be very fair with all his people. Lewin certainly would gain by the change. As for Dom Anselm, he knew perfectly that Roger would never need a priest, for—a strange fact even in those dreadful days—he was an open scoffer. At the same time, the scoundrel was rather tired of the business. Among men-at-arms it was not lucrative, though their superstition enjoined a certain amount of respect for him. He knew a little about the rude medicine of that time, had some skill in simples, and he would, he thought, join Roger as a chirurgeon provided that all went well.

So he and Lewin laid their plans together.

Dom Anselm slept on the cool side of the wall, all undisturbed by the noise around. The appearance of the courtyard had quite altered by this time. Sloping scaffolds of wood, connected by plank galleries, ran up to the walls and made it possible to instantly concentrate a large force of men upon any given point which should be attacked.

The fantastic arms of the mangonels and trebuchets, and other slinging instruments rose grimly above the battlements. A great crane upon the top of a tower, slung up piles of rocks and barrels of Greek fire with steady industry. Shields of wood, covered with damp hide and pierced with loop-holes, frowned on the top of the battlements towards the outside world.

Great heaps of a sort of hand grenade, made of wicker work and full of a foul concoction of sulphur and pitch, were arranged at intervals, and iron braziers, standing on tripod legs, were dotted here and there, so that the soldiers could at once obtain a light for a pitch barrel or grenade.

A large copper gong with a wooden club to beat it was being fitted to a stand of ash-wood. The harsh reverberations of this horrid instrument could be heard above the din of any fight, and made a better signal than trumpets.

Amid all the metallic noises, the dishonoured priest slept sweetly. He was roused by two startling events.

The first was this. With a great clatter a soldier rode into the courtyard. His horse was foam-flecked, his furniture and arms all powdered grey with dust. He swore with horrid oaths that he had one great overpowering desire, and that not to be denied. It was beer he said that he wanted, and would have before he spoke a single word. He bellowed for beer. When they brought it him, in a crowd, for he was a scout with news from the Norwich road, he gurgled his content and shouted his news.

Lord Roger had pressed on with great speed, and was now close at hand. Probably as evening fell that day, certainly during that night, his force would camp round the walls. They took him away to Fulke's chamber, where that worthy, who had been up all night, was snatching a little sleep. They thronged round him clamouring for more news.

The Serf

Dom Anselm once more sat him down in the cool shade of the draw-well, this time with a feeble pretence at reading in his dirty drink-stained little breviary. It was curious to see how early habit reasserted itself in this way.

Then the second startling event occurred.

There came a burst of distant cheering, an explosion of fierce cries at the gates, and a little mob of men-at-arms rushed into the bailey, followed by half a dozen sentinels with pikes in their hands.

In the middle of the crowd a man stood bound, dressed in a leathern jacket, and the soldiers were beating him over the head with the shafts of their pikes. His face ran with blood and there was an awful stare of horror in his eyes.

So Hyla came back to Hilgay.

At the gate of the castle they had halted him, with many oaths, and turned his head towards a tree, from one of whose branches hung the naked swollen corpse of Elgifu.

Dom Anselm lurched up from the side of the well and shouldered his way through the press. Here again was his dramatic opportunity. Face to face with the prisoner, he stopped short and spat venomously into his face. With that, Dom Anselm also passes out of the story.

They held Hyla and buffeted him, while the soldiers from all parts of the castle works ran towards the courtyard.

They came running down the slanting bridges leading from the walls, and their feet made a noise like thunder on the echoing boards. The cooks came out of the kitchens, the serfs from the stables, until there was a great bawling, shouting crowd, struggling and fighting to get a look at the captive.

None were louder in their menace than the serfs.

Some zealous soul, inspired by uncontrollable excitement, feeling the curious need of personal action that often comes to an excitable nature labouring under a sudden nerve stress, got him to the chamber at the foot of Outfangthef and fell to pulling lustily at the castle bell.

Suddenly, with the swiftness of a mechanical trick, a deep stillness of voice and gesture fell upon the tumult. It was as though some wizard had made his spell and turned them all to stone. Every eye turned towards Outfangthef and a lane opened among the people. Fulke was seen coming down the steps, and behind him was his sister, the Lady Alice de la Bourne.

The lady stayed on her coign at the head of the stairway, palpitating, and he came slowly down towards the prisoner. In a second they were face to face.

Twice Fulke put his hand to the pommel of his dagger, and twice he let it fall away. He said nothing, but his sinister eyes looked steadily at Hyla till the serf dropped his head before the gaze of his victim's son, so hard, bitter, and cruel it was.

At last Fulke turned to the soldiers: "Take him to the guard-room," he said, "and keep him in safety there until I send you word. As for the rest of you, get you back to work, for there is not a moment to lose. Let the portcullis fall and heave the drawbridge up, keep station all of you. I promise you a merry sight with that"—he pointed to Hyla—"ere long. He will cry meculpee with his heart's black blood."

He saw the two squires and Lewin among the crowd, and nodded that they should come to him. Then, turning, he went with them into the tower, to his own room again.

To be frank, there was very little drama in that meeting. One might have expected drama, Romance would certainly require it, but Fulke was not the nature to rise to the occasion. He lacked temperament. He would have better pleased his men if he had made more display. Indeed, as they separated into little groups and discussed the incident, Dom Anselm was discovered as the hero of the moment. Holy Church had distinctly scored.

When the Baron reached his room he proceeded to discuss the method of Hyla's execution with his friends.

He wanted, he said, to make a very public thing of it, indeed he was quite determined to hang him from the very top of Outfangthef. At the same time that was far too easy a death.

They turned their four evil brains to the question of torture, a grim conclave, and, curiously enough, it was the keenest and most refined intelligence which invented the worst atrocities. Lewin proposed things more horrible than Fulke could ever have thought of. They applauded him for his very serviceable knowledge of anatomy. The pain of Hyla, it was eventually settled, was to last till he could bear no more, and he should hang from the Tower at the end. With that decision made they fell drinking, for Hyla was not to suffer until after the mid-day meal.

The two men chosen to inflict the torture were two swarthy foreign scoundrels from Mirebeau, men who knew no earthly scruple. About two in the afternoon a little procession started to the guard-house.

Lewin's interest in the proceedings was already over. He did not join them. He had suggested various tortures, it was a mental exercise which amused him, but that was all. Nothing would have induced him to watch his own horrible brutalities being inflicted on the victim.

He threaded his way among the pens of lowing cattle and the litter of war material to a tower in the forework, and presently, as the long afternoon waned lazily away, his quick eyes caught sight of a clump of spears, a mile away, on the edge of the wood.

By half the night was over, Hilgay was invested. All round the walls camp-fires glowed in the dark, and snatches of song in chorus could be heard, or a trumpet blaring orders. Now and again the guards upon the battlements would hear the thunder of a horse's hoofs, as some officer or galloper went *ventre à terre* down the village street, and a few random arrows went singing after him.

Every one anxiously awaited the day.

CHAPTER XVII

"So when this corruptible shall have put on in corruption, and this mortal shall have put on immortality; then shall be brought to pass the saying that is written, Death is swallowed up in victory. O death, where is thy sting? O grave, where is thy victory?"

Huber, the man-at-arms, went slowly round the battlements as the sun rose. He was in full panoply of war time. A steel cap was on his head, and he wore a supple coat of leathern thongs laced together, and made stronger by thin plates of steel at the shoulder and upper part of the arms.

He had a long shield on his left arm, a cavalry shield notched at the top for a lance. He was inspecting the defences, and he carried this great shield to protect himself from any chance shaft from the enemy, for he made a conspicuous mark every now and again against the sky line.

The two squires followed him, well content to learn of such a veteran. He was pure soldier; nothing escaped him. He saw that each archer, with his huge painted long-bow, had his bracer and shooting glove ready. He found three sharp-shooters had only one small piece of wax among them, and sent for more, cursing them for improvident fools.

The Serf

When he came to an arbalestrier his eye brightened at the sight of the weapon—by far the deadliest of that day, despite the praisers of the English yew—which he loved. He tested the strong double cords with the moulinet, inspected the squat thick quarrels which lay in large leather quivers, hung to the masonry by pegs, and saw that each steel-lined groove was clean and shining.

The man's eyes gleamed with satisfaction as he went his rounds. "Look you, sir," he said to Brian de Burgh, "we are well set up in this fortalice. Never a thing is lacking! Nary castle from here to London is so well found." He pointed to a pile of brassarts, the arm-guards used by the archers, which lay by a trough full of long steel-headed arrows, with bristles of goose and pigeon feathers.

"This is a powerful good creature in attack," he continued, pointing to a heap of lime. "A little water and a dipper to fling the mess with, and a-burneth out a man's eyes within the hour."

A serf came clambering up the wooden scaffolds which led to the walls. He carried seven or eight long ash wands. At the end of each hung a long pennon of linen. He gave them to Huber.

"What are these, Huber?" said young Richard Ferville, as the soldier took them.

"It is a plan I saw at Arques," he answered, "Tête Rouge was head bowyer there. *Ma foi*, and he could shoot you a good shoot! At Arques, sir, as you may know, strong winds blow from the sea on one side, though 'tis miles inland, and on the other the wind cometh down the valley from Envermeau. Now but a little breeze will send an arrow from the mark. A man who can shoot a good shoot from tower or wall must ever watch the wind. Now Tête-Rouge was a ship-man once, and watched wind in the manner of use. But he could not train his men to judge a quarter-wind as he was able. So he raised pennons like these. 'Tis but a ribbon and every breeze moveth it, so the long-bow-men may shoot the straighter."

As he spoke the archers were fixing the thin poles in staples, which had been prepared for them.

"Holá!" cried Brian de Burgh, "the bastard's flag goes up." Even as he spoke a distant flourish of tuckets came down the morning wind. They leant out over the crenelets and strained their eyes down the hill, fenwards.

A flag hung from a tall pole, which stood before a white pavilion.

"A banneret!" said Huber. "The bastard has grown in roods and perches of late. Can you read it for me, Master Richard?"

The squire made a funnel of his hands and gazed at the flag. "A moline cross, if I see aright," he said, "but it does not matter. Roger's flag eke his coat-armour, are what he has a mind to use, not what he useth by any right of birth."

"Can'st see what they are doing out by the carts—by the edge of the orchard?"

"Yes, sir. They be working on the mantelets, and anon they will wheel them up to protect those who would raise a palisade on the moat's edge. But come, Master Richard, we must be on the rounds. Much must be looked to. Now look you, Sir Brian, in a siege the hoards are your defender's chief stand-by. Now we are going into each one, for it is in those defences that we must trust in time of attack. When your hoards are breached, then your castle is like to fall."

He spoke with the technical assurance of a veteran—a sergeant-major respectfully imparting his own riper knowledge to a brace of subalterns.

The "hoards" were wooden structures, little pent-house forts, run out from the curtains, standing on great beams which fitted into holes in the masonry. From behind the breastwork of thick wood the archers could shoot with a freedom—this way and that—

which was denied them by the long oblique openings in the wall itself. They commanded all points.

The group walked out along the narrow gangway, which stretched out over the black moat below, and entered the temporary fort of wood. It was built for the accommodation of four or five men, sharp-shooters, who were practically safe from everything but heavy artillery fire from mangonel and catapult.

They surveyed the scene before them in silence. The morning had risen clear, calm, and hot. For weeks the morning had been just as this was, and they had strolled along the battlements to catch the cool air and sharpen an early appetite. But on those other days the meadows beyond the moat, which ran to the forest edge, had been silent and empty, save for herds of swine and red peaceful cattle. Now, but two hundred yards away, scarce more than that it seemed in the clear keen air of dawn, were the tents, the dying fires, the litter and stir, of a great hostile camp.

The lines of men, horses, and carts, stretched away right and left in a long curve, till Outfangthef hid them on one side, and the gateway towers, with their pointed roofs, upon the other.

They could hear the trumpets, the hammers of the carpenters, a confused shouting of orders, and the hum of active men, as the besiegers began to prepare the manifold engines of attack, which—perhaps before night fell—would be creeping slowly towards the walls of Hilgay.

That great low shed which lay upon the ground like a monstrous tortoise, would presently creep slowly towards them, foot by foot, until it reached the edge of the moat, and the men beneath it would build their great fence of logs and empty carts of rubbish into the sullen waters.

They could see men upon the sloping roofs, gradually sloping from a central ridge, men like great flies, nailing tanned hides over the beams. The sound of tapping hammers reached them from the work which should be protective of Greek fire and burning tar from above.

And against the light green of the meadow-lands, and the darker olive of the thick forest trees, the many colours of pennons, the glint of sunlight upon arms, gave the animation of the scene an added quality of picturesqueness. How "decorative" it all was! how vivid and complete a picture! And yet how stern and sinister in meaning.

"Bella premunt hostilia,

Da robur, fer auxilium."

The soldiers were silent as they leaned out over the pent-house. Huber crossed himself, for the chapel bell began to toll down below in the fortress.

The squires left the works and descended to the bailey. Huber remained on the wall. From where he stood he could see all over the castle. Such of the garrison as were not on guard or employed in active preparation straggled slowly over the grass towards the chapel door. Some of the serfs followed, the man-at-arms could easily distinguish their characteristic dress.

He turned curiously pale beneath his bronze. Then his eyes turned towards the noble tower Outfangthef, and presently fixed themselves on a low iron door, between two buttresses, which was nearly below the level of the yard, and must be reached by a few old mildewed steps.

His eyes remained fixed upon the archway of the door, and his face became full of a great gloom and horror.

The Serf

The sentinels passed and re-passed him as he stared down below with set pale features. At length he turned and entered one of the hoards. The angle of the side hid him from view of the men upon the walls.

There Huber knelt down and prayed for the serf who had saved his life on Wilfrith Mere, and now lay deep down behind that iron door.

The strong man beat his breast and bowed his head. As he prayed, with unwonted tears in his eyes, he heard the distant silver tinkle that meant the elevation of The Host. He bowed still lower with his hands crossed upon his breast.

For to this rugged and lonely worshipper also, the message was coming that all men are brothers.

"*Suscipe, sancte Pater,—hanc immaculatam Hostiam,*" that was what Anselm was saying down there in the chapel; and He who heard the one offering would not despise the other, a broken and a contrite heart.

And so farewell to Huber.

In a dark place, under the ground, full of filth and rats, Hyla lay dying in the crucet hûs. It is not necessary to say how they had used him.

He was not unconscious, though now and again the brain would fly from the poor maimed body, but the swoon never lasted long.

In the long and awful night, in that black tomb, with no noise but the pattering of the rats, what did he think of?

I think there were two great emotions in his heart. He prayed very earnestly to God, that he might die and be at peace, and he cried a great deal that he could not say good-bye to Gruach. The unmarried cannot know how bitterly a man wants his wife in trouble. Hyla kept sobbing and moaning her name all night.

The second day, though he never knew a day had gone down there, they had but little time to torture him, and after half an hour of unbearable agony he was left alone in silence. No one but an enormously strong man could have lived for half as long.

Still in his brain there was no thought of martyrdom, and none of the exaltation that it might have given. Although he prayed, and believed indeed, that God heard him, his imaginative faculties were not now acute enough to help him to any ghostly comfort. Continually he whimpered for Gruach, until at length he sank into a last stupor.

At last, at the end of the afternoon, his two torturers came and unbound the maimed thing they had made.

"It is the end now, Hyla," said one of them, "very soon and it will be over. They are all a-waiting, and my Lord Roger Bigot of Norwich has given us an hour's truce, while we kill you, you dog!"

They untied the thongs, and lifted him from the cruel stones. One of them gave him a horn of wine, so that he might have a little strength. It revived him somewhat, and they half led, half carried him up the stairs. Up and on they went, on that last terrible journey, until the lantern, which was carried by a soldier in front of them, began to pale before rich lights of sunset, which poured in at the loop-holes in the stairway wall.

They were climbing up Outfangthef.

The fresh airs of evening played about them. After the stench of the *oubliette*, it was like heaven to Hyla.

They passed up and up, among the chirping birds, until a little ill-fitting wooden door, through the chinks of which the light poured like water, showed their labour was at an end. The serf's spirits rose enormously. At last! At last! Death was at hand. At this

The Serf

moment of supreme excitement, he nerved himself to be a man. The occasion altered his whole demeanour. Almost by a miracle his submissive attitude dropped from him. His dull eyes flashed, his broken body became almost straight. The heavy, vacuous expression fled from his face never to return, and his nostrils curved in disdain, and with pride at this thing he had done.

It was better to be hanged on a tower like this than on the tree at the castle gate, he thought as the little door opened.

They came out upon the platform in the full blaze of the setting sun. Far, far below, the smiling woods lay happily, and the rooks called to each other round the tree-tops. The river wound its way into the fen like a silver ribbon. Peace and sweetness lay over all the land.

Hyla turned his weary head and took one last look at this beautiful sunset England.

A great cheering came from below as the execution party came out on the battlements, a fierce roar of execration.

While they were fitting his neck with the rope, Hyla looked down. The castle was spread below him like a map, very vivid in the bright light. Hundreds of tiny white faces were turned towards him. Outside the walls he saw a great camp with tents and huts, among which fires were just being lit to cook the evening meal.

At last, on the edge of the coping they let him kneel down for prayer. Lord Fulke had not yet sounded the signal, down in the courtyard, when they should swing him out.

He did not pray, but looked out over the lovely country-side with keen brave eyes. Freedom was very, very near. Freedom at last! The soldiers could not understand his rapt face, it frightened them. As he gazed, his eye fell on a round tower at the far end of the defences. Down the side of the tower a man was descending by means of a rope. Although at this distance he appeared quite small, something in the dress or perhaps in the colour of the hair proclaimed it to be Lewin. The executioners saw him also.

"God!" said one of them. "There goes our minter to Roger. The black hound!"

He bent over the edge of the abyss and shouted frantically to the crowd below, but he could convey no meaning to them. The little moving figure on the wall had disappeared by now, but a group of men standing at the moat-side showed that he was expected.

Hyla saw all this with little interest. He was perfectly calm, and all his pain had left him. Already he was at peace.

A keen blast from a trumpet sounded in the courtyard below, and came snarling up to them.

There was a sudden movement, and then the two hosts of the besiegers and besieged saw a black swinging figure sharply outlined against the ruddy evening sky.

Justice had been done. But may we not suppose that the death notes of that earthly horn swelled and grew in the poor serf's ears, pulsing louder and more gloriously triumphant, until he knew them for the silver trumpets of the Heralds of Heaven coming to welcome him?

Deo Gratias.

THE END

Printed in Great Britain
by Amazon.co.uk, Ltd.,
Marston Gate.